If Only They Knew

Written by Jessica Sherrell

Copyright © Jessica Sherrell, 2020

Cover image: © Visionary Tactics

ISBN-13: 978-0-578-23335-2

Published by Chocolate Readings
www.chocolatereadings.com

Publisher's Note

This book is dedicated to...

———●●———

To all of my loved ones who are no longer with me here on Earth.

Aubrey Gracelynn Glass (my rainbow baby), Jessie James Walden (my father), Eloise M. Taylor (my grandmother), Shamar Walden (my first cousin), and Carrie Mae Walden (my grandmother). Thank you for loving me and unconditionally. Your legacy lives through me.

&

This book is also dedicated to all of my Mississippi readers. Because of you, I am able to bring light on the true Dirty Souf.

If Only They Knew

Chapter 1

"Well, Mrs. Jackson. I got some news. I am not going to say if it's good or bad because it's all up to how you take it," the doctor said, as she walked in the room with her eyes fixated on the clipboard.

Fourteen-year-old Mia sat on the examining table in a white gown feeling optimistic. She let her feet dangle over the sides of the examining table while her mother, Mrs. Jackson, sat adjacent to her in a black leather chair reading a magazine. Mrs. Jackson's demeanor was cool and calm.

After waiting over 45 minutes, Mia and her mother was over waiting for the doctor to confirm what she and her mom already knew.

"Mrs. Jackson, Tamia is pregnant," the doctor said with no emotions at all.

Dr. Ramsey was seasoned. She had been practicing for over 30 years. She had seen her share of young, pregnant teenage girls. To her, all of them were in way over their heads.

In Dr. Ramsey's past years, she was employed at a non-profit where she worked with adolescent girls on sex education and teenage pregnancy. She gave up that, "she has to save the world cape" a long time ago. She used to tell her colleagues, "Those young girls never listen. The more you try to save them the more they are in heat. Just like dogs. They won't stop until they lie down and get up with fleas."

Dr. Ramsey looked to be in her late 50's. She was white and looked to be aging quickly. She wore different wigs due to having a hair condition called Alopecia. She spent long nights in the ER and often abandoned her own daughters who resented her for not spending time with them.

"PREGNANT!" Mia and her mother both screamed in unison. The room seemed to go completely silent. Aside from Dr. Ramsey rambling the test results, Mia was in complete shock. Here she was, fourteen years old, coming to the ER thinking she had the flu. Instead, this lady with a twisted wig is telling her she's pregnant. Mia wanted to say some dumb stuff like "how could this be?" She knew how but at that moment all she could think was HOW?

Mrs. Jackson must've thought the same thing because she asked Dr. Ramsey what Mia was thinking.

"But how? There must be some type of mistake. This can't be," Mrs. Jackson said while shaking her head in disbelief.

"Mrs. Jackson, I know there's no easy way to handle your daughter being sexually active but well.... the fact is the results are 99.99% accurate."

Mia sucked her teeth.

Mrs. Jackson gave Mia an intense stare.

At that very moment, Mia wanted to shrink. Not the "honey I shrunk the kids," type of shrink; but, the "how stupid could I be," type of shrink. For weeks, she had been feeling nauseated, running a high fever, runny nose, and fatigue. All the symptoms of the flu, right?

Wrong!

Mia was pregnant. Although she had been in some tight situations before, this by far took the cake. All she could think was, *Oh shit! Could this be real? Am I pregnant?* Mia was devastated.

"Dr. Ramsey, you must see this type of stuff every day but is there any way to tell how far along she is?" Mrs. Jackson asked with pure confusion.

"Honestly, it's too early to tell."

As if she was looking for the answers, Dr. Ramsey turned and asked Mia with her eyes still fixated on her clipboard. "Mia how long have you been feeling like you had the flu?"

Mia shrugged her shoulders.

"Answer her!" Mrs. Jackson yelled. "You have no right to sit here and not give us no answers. So, how long have you been feeling like you had the flu?"

Mia let her head drop. She honestly didn't know. She was annoyed at the fact that her answer wasn't good enough. She was used to lying and if a lie is what they wanted, a lie is what she was willing to give.

"About two weeks," she said softly.

"Based off that Mrs. Jackson, she's probably between three to four weeks but there's no way to be for sure without a sonogram or blood test."

"This is ridiculous. Get dressed and let's go," Mrs. Jackson spat.

"I will have the receptionist give you all some pamphlets about your options and you can schedule a follow up for four weeks." Dr. Ramsey took off her gloves, washed her hands, and left.

As Mia got dressed, her mother waited for her in the waiting room. She purposely took her time dressing because she already knew what was up.

See, Mia's mother was your typical African American mother. Mrs. Jackson stood 5'6, weighed about 190lbs, brown caramel skin with a mole in the crease of her right eye. She was pretty average in appearance, but she made up for what she lacked with attitude.

Mrs. Jackson didn't play either. A lot of the stuff some kids got away with Mia didn't. She was well known in the neighborhood as Mrs. G., which is short for Grace, and she prided herself on making sure Mia wasn't like most of the neighborhood girls. She felt what her and Mia's father lacked financially, they could pour into her character.

Mia dripped with swag. She always had the latest gear, jewelry, and gadgets. Mrs. Jackson had her taking piano, karate, and dance classes to make sure

Mia was too busy to get into the neighborhood's activities.

And now she's pregnant.

Mia slowly turned the examiner room's doorknob to surprisingly find her mother with tears rolling down her eyes. If that didn't make Mia's emotions worse, what else would? She's never really seen her mother cry; especially, not because of something she did. Her mother was always so strong and rarely ever showed her true emotions.

On the ride home, neither of them said a word. Mia purposely stared out the window. She took in the sights like she was preparing for doom's day.

Mia was from a small city right outside of the capital in Mississippi. The great state that birthed Oprah, David Banner, Ike Turner, Brandy & Ray J, and so many more.

It was a hot sunny day during mid-June in 2005. As they rode in mental silence, 107.1 echoed "Be Without You" by Mary J. Blige. Mia saw kids playing, people washing their cars for the local Sunday drives, and life seemed to still be moving.

Not Mia's!

Mia's life seemed to be at a complete standstill. To make matters worse, Mrs. Jackson wasn't saying a word. Mia was more prepared for her to curse her out. She felt she deserved that much, but that didn't happen. Just the tunes of Mary J. matching her mood.

Every now and then, Mia would peep at her mother through her peripheral to see if she was looking at her. Mrs. Jackson just drove her white 2002 Toyota with her eyes eagerly on the road and her hands strategically at 10 & 2.

They slowly pulled into their modest one-story garage and Mrs. Jackson turned the engine off. She turned to Mia with the most disappointed yet concerned voice Mia had ever heard from her mother and said, "Mia, this has to stay between me and you. That means you can't tell your father. Not until we figure this thing out. We will; however, have to tell Grandma Rose."

This was the most expected unexpected statement ever because this how it was in Mia's household. Everybody had secrets, so this was nothing new.

Mia lived with her parents, Grace, and Tim, but her grandma, Rose, ran the show.

"What are you going to tell her?" Mia asked while strategically avoiding eye contact.

"I am going to tell her that her fourteen-year-old granddaughter is pregnant. What else should I tell her? Or, would you rather tell her?"

"I..I...I don't know. I guess you can tell her."

"You're out here playing and acting grown. I should make you tell her. We are not telling your father because this would kill him. He thinks the world of you and as much as it hurts me, I rather carry this secret for the both of us. Mia, you have truly disappointed me. We work so hard to make sure you live a good life. You could easily be living in the hood, on welfare, and struggling but open your naïve eyes and look around you. HOLD YOUR HEAD UP AND LOOK! Look at your neighborhood, look at the clothes you are wearing, look at the car you're riding in, and look at all the privileges you have. Do you want to be somebody's baby momma or worst walking around eighth grade with a baby in your belly?"

Mia simply shook her head. She had nothing to say. Mainly because she wanted, what she considered an integration, to end.

"Tell me what you want because obviously, my way isn't working. What do you want Mia?"

"You can tell Grandma Rose," Mia replied.

"Fine. Not a word of this to your father until your grandmother and I can figure this mess out."

They got out of the car and seemed to be on one accord. Mia wondered though. Her mother never asked any questions about her sexual experience. She didn't ask "who, what, when and where." And truthfully Mia was happy.

Thing's could've easily gone left if her mother had asked. Mia's secrets ran deeper than she believed her mother could handle. If she had to tell her mother, the raw brutal truth, Mia would have to tell her more than how she got pregnant. She would have to tell her the innocence she thought her daughter had was a false perception of their reality.

Chapter 2

ays seemed to move in slow motion. And
just like Mrs. Jackson said, not a word was
mentioned to Mia's dad. Mia sat in her room,
planning to go outside to get some fresh air. While
trying on clothes her mind began to build a slight
curiosity about how her young frame would look
carrying a baby. She poked her stomach out and
rubbed her hands over her belly. That thought was
quickly wiped away from her mind when Mrs. Jackson
peaked her head into the room and said, "Get up! Your
grandmother is outside."

Mia instantly jumped as if she was caught
stealing. She stood up and slid on her yellow sandals.
She felt sick. She felt nauseated and queasy. Mia wasn't
sure she felt this way because of her pregnancy or the
fact that she was about to face her biggest challenge-
her grandmother.

Mia's grandmother was intimidating. She was
the type of person that could build you up but with one
quick slash of the tongue cut your whole existence in
half. Grandma Rose was a story within herself. The
love of Mia's life but the meanest, firmest yet loving
lady you'll ever get to meet. She was the funds of the
family. If anything needed to be handled, she was the
go-to person. Mia's friends often joked that Grandma

Rose sold drugs. It sounded cool to Mia, so she rolled with it.

Grandma Rose, in her prime and her season, was *that* lady. Every Cadillac you can drive, decked out three-story house, Rolex on her wrist, and as clean as a first lady. Grandma Rose owned several daycares around the city. It was called My Rose Daycare. She was Mrs. Jackson's mother and granted she wasn't the best mother to her children growing up, she made it up with her grandkids, especially Mia. Being the oldest grandchild, Mia got a lot of advantages. Spoiled to say the least.

Mia sat on the passenger side of Grandma Rose's all-black Cadillac sedan looking intensely straight forward while Grandma Rose sat silently flipping through her newspaper. *What is she doing? Does she know this is serious? How could she be reading at a time like this?* Mia thought.

Grandma Rose continued to look straight ahead as she interrupted the silence with her stern intimidating voice, "Mia, don't you know there's an epidemic of AIDS going on." There was a long pause. *Was this a rhetorical question,* Mia thought. Grandma Rose continued, "You're just fourteen and you are having sex without protection. Do you know AIDS can kill you, little girl?" This time her voice raised from stern to anger. "Who is this boy you out here opening your legs for? Have we not taught you anything? You have no idea what's in store for you."

Mia's nervousness set in. Her mother hasn't once asked her about who her baby daddy was. It wasn't like she didn't know but there were some underlying things that she wouldn't dare tell her grandmother.

———————◆•◆———————

Mia and her best friend, Sky, sat in Sky's mother's 1999 Buick Regal. Sky's mother often gave her the car to make grocery store runs or some small errands that she, herself, was too busy to do. On this particular day, Mia and Sky decided to do a little joyriding. It was right after school one Friday and Sky convinced her mother to let her get the car to go to the library. In reality, the library wasn't even on the agenda for Mia and Sky. Sky had previously met this guy named Troy. She and Troy had been messing around for a few weeks. It wasn't long before Mia persuaded Troy to introduce her to his friend, Drew.

Troy and Drew lived in Presidential Hills projects, which was nowhere near where Sky and Mia lived. They were the neighborhood drug dealers who sat around Troy's auntie's house selling weed and prescription drugs. Troy was ninteen years old. He stood 5'11, with dark skin complexion, low cut fade, and weighed about 180 lbs. of which was pure lean muscle. He looked like he could bench press 150 lbs. with his eyes closed.

Drew was also nineteen, stood 6ft tall, light skin complexion, and rocked his hair in braids. He often took pride in his hair and wore different types of designs to show off his style. The brother was like heaven to Mia. When she first met him, she couldn't stop staring at his pearly white teeth.

Mia remembered the first time that she saw him like it was yesterday. Drew came outside dripping in swag. He had on dark blue baggy jeans, a white t-shirt, light blue jean jacket, and some all-white air force ones.

"Sup shawty. Why ya'll cuties not at school?" Drew asked as he leaned into the passenger door.

Mia seductively turned her head to him with her lips full of lip gloss and said, "School is out baby boy."

"Oh word, well come err and let me rap with you for a minute," he replied while opening her car door.

Drew stared at Mia's ass, as she exited the car. She felt him watching so she added an extra prance to her walk to draw him in. They went into Troy's auntie's house and sat in the living room. Mia instantly noticed that the house reeked of weed smoke. The smell was so potent that she had to put her shirt over her nose.

Drew began to laugh. "Dang, the loud pack is kind of loud, huh? Let me open the window and spray some air freshener for you."

"How can ya'll stay in here like this?" Mia asked with her nose turned up.

"Baby, we're used to it. This is like the smell of Pine-sol for us," Drew added.

"I see," Mia retorted as she looked around the junky house. It looked like the house hadn't been cleaned in weeks. There were cigarette butts on the table that were supposed to be in the ashtray, dishes piled up in the sink, stains on the carpet, and old worn-in couches. Mia barely wanted to sit down when she walked in.

"You alright?" Drew asked as he noticed her facial expression.

"Nah, I'm good."

"So what's up? Your girl Sky has told me a lot about you."

"Oh really? Knowing Sky she probably exaggerated a lot."

"Honestly, everything she told me is true. You're beautiful but bougie, too. I like that shit!"

Mia blushed. After she was able to ease up a little and not focus so much on her surroundings, she found herself laughing and blushing the entire day.

After their initial encounter, Mia and Drew would stay up and talk for hours. It's like they were practically inseparable. Any chance she could, she would ride with Sky to go see him. Sometimes she would go alone, and he would pay for her a cab. Of course, she would tell her mother she was studying at

Sky's for some big project or hard homework assignment. Although, there was a five year age difference, Drew made Mia feel grown. Like a woman who should be desired.

After spending time and talking for almost a month, Drew finally made his move. "Yo ma. We been talking for a minute nah and you know a nigga feeling the shit out of yo sexy ass. I'm saying though, I am trying to make you Mrs. Drew," he said while they sat on his twin size bed.

Drew shared a room with his younger brother and figured this was the perfect time to take things to the next level since his mother nor brother were home. Mia looked around the room with her palms shaky. She noticed the Power Ranger wallpaper and clothes all over Drew's bed. Drew noticed it so he tried a little harder.

"You know I wanted you from the first time I laid eyes on ya. You was looking right with them Baby Phat jeans on wearing your hair in a wrap. Yea, a nigga remembers all of that shit. Real talk. You got me falling in love and I ain't never been in love."

Mia felt flattered. Or maybe vulnerable. Either way, she felt the sincerity in his voice. She considered giving in to Drew, but she was very much still a virgin. Her and Sky use to act older but her innocence was very much intact, and she wasn't sure she was ready to let it go just yet. Then again, she wanted to be Drew's girl. Even though they acted like it, truth was, she wasn't. That's because he always encouraged her to keep things between them quiet. He used to say that her mother wouldn't like him because he sold drugs. In reality, it was that and he was much older.

Hearing Drew say the big "L" word made Mia feel safe. She felt comfortable. And ready. Grandma Rose always told her what rape was like and she knew that this wasn't what Grandma Rose explained. Anxiously, Mia said, "Okay, I want to, too."

Drew's eyes lit up like Christmas day. He began kissing her and fondling her small A-cups as if they were D-cups. He let his hands run down to the button of her pants. Mia unconsciously jumped. This was foreign for her. It felt so strange to have someone touching her like this. She was nervous but she wanted it. If she had to lose her virginity, she wanted it to be with Drew.

"It's okay, Ma. I got chu," Drew said in lust. Drew laid Mia down on his bed. He quickly began to take off her fitted jeans. Mainly because he didn't want her to change her mind and he darn sure didn't want his mother to come home. Mia was so inexperienced she didn't even ask for a condom. Before she knew it, she was wincing in pain. The penetration hit her body like a voltage. It was nothing like the movies made it seem.

"*Oooo..... AAAHHH..... Ummm,*" Mia grunted.

Drew was in bliss. He thought Mia was too but in reality, she was in pain. Mia still had on her blue Vneck t-shirt, but her panties and pants were on the floor. She wanted to so badly to tell him to stop but she didn't want him to think she was just another young girl. Drew kept thrusting with his head down and lips by her ear saying, "Owee Mama, this shit is good. Are you going to be Mrs. Drew? I want this forever. You hear me."

Mia never said a word she just kept grunting and wincing in pain. Fifteen minutes went by, but it seemed like an hour to Mia. Once Drew was done, he went and got Mia a wet towel. Too sore to stand up, Drew had to wipe the sex off of her. Not to be rude, he knew his mother would soon be home, so Mia had to go. And just like that, the bliss was over.

———————•◦•———————

Mia had to think quickly on her feet. Grandma Rose was waiting. She wanted answers and she wanted them today.

Mia quickly responded, "It's just some boy I met. We don't even attend the same school." Mia didn't want Grandma Rose asking questions and she knew by saying they went to different schools the chances would be slim of them seeing each other.

"So you out here meeting boys outside of school. Grace ought to be ashamed of herself not watching you like that," Grandma Rose protested. Mia gave Grandma Rose a once over. It sounded like Grandma Rose was pointing the finger at her mother. If she was, Mia was ready to ride that wave. Mia wanted fewer eyes on her as possible. She didn't want Grandma Rose or her mother asking her a million questions and she for sure didn't want them to find out about Drew. She hadn't even told him yet and she had no clue how he would respond.

"Mia, I am going to clean your mother's mess up once again. You are not having this baby. Ya hear me! You are too young and too smart to be around here carrying some baby. You deserve so much more for your future."

Grandma Rose continued to go on about Mia's life. Mia was slightly upset that no one asked her how she felt. No one even asked if she wanted a baby. She felt helpless. Mia got out of Grandma Rose's car tearful. She ran to her room and cried herself to sleep.

Chapter 3

*M*ia woke up to the smell of eggs and bacon cooking in the kitchen. She sluggishly turned over to look at the clock on her nightstand and to her surprise it was 10:30 a.m. She had almost slept her Saturday away. She needed to get up and meet with Sky. They had so much catching up to do and she hadn't even told her about all the drama that had been going on. Mia scurried to shower and quickly got dressed. She wore a long blue and white striped dress. The dress fitted perfectly. Not too tight but it disguised her small bump that was forming. She pulled her long bronze hair in a messy bun and slid on a pair of thong sandals. Mia was a beautiful girl. She was about 5'5, 130lbs, brown-mocha skin, with a slim physique. She often reminded people of a younger version of Angela Simmons.

She didn't need makeup or any mascara. Her long dark black eyelashes naturally curled. She almost always wore lip gloss. And today was no different. She applied the thick gloss to her lips and followed the aroma of the food.

Mia walked into the kitchen to find her father, Tim, cooking breakfast. "There's my baby girl. How you doing this morning?" Tim asked as he kissed her forehead. Mia had been trying to avoid her father, as much as possible.

Tim was a cross-country state truck driver. He was rarely at home during the week. This often brought on tension between him and Grace. Because Tim wasn't home much, Grace was a fulltime wife and mother. Grace resented the fact that Tim got to work while she stayed home. Tim felt if he was keeping a roof over his wife's and daughter's head, food on the table, and Mia in every activity that she wanted to be in, then he was doing what a man was supposed to.

Grace and Tim had been married for fourteen years. When Grace found out she was pregnant, she wasn't too thrilled. She had just started nursing school and was seeking to start a career in the nursing field. Tim, however, was ecstatic. As soon as he found out Grace was having a girl, he told any and everyone. The problem was Tim wasn't particularly prepared financially and mentally for a baby. At the time, Tim was working an oil rig doing construction. He was making very little money but working overtime. Not to mention, he was a lady's man. Tim was known for having a woman or two stored away when he wanted to have some fun. Grace knew about the women, but she turned a blind eye when she found out she was pregnant.

Not Grandma Rose, though. Once Grandma Rose heard about Tim's infidelities from one of the parents at one of her daycares, she wasted no time and arranged them to get married right in her living room day, a before Tamia Gracelyn Jackson was born.

Grandma Rose bought the ring and hired the pastor. She even made herself a bridesmaid.

"How you been? I feel like we haven't talked in a while. What's new?" Tim asked. Mia was a daddy's girl and she knew whatever her little heart desired Tim would provide.

"I've been okay, Daddy. I have been kind of sad because it seems like I have been in the house since the summer started. Can you drop me off at Sky's house?"

"Sure, once you sit down and eat breakfast with your old man, I will drop you off on my way to Home Depot."

Mia hurriedly ate. She didn't want her dad looking through her and most importantly she didn't want him to notice how round her face was becoming.

"Dang baby, slow down. I can make you some more."

"No daddy I am full. I am trying to get to Sky's because we are going to have a girls' day out."

Mia wasn't lying. She and Sky were planning to catch up and do what they did best and that is, "whatever the hell they wanted to."

"Well before I drop you off, you'll have to talk to me first."

"Come on, dad. I have to get to Sky's or I am going to miss all the fun."

"Trust me. Sky won't leave you out. So, tell me what has been going on while I am away?"

Mia looked confused. She didn't know what her father knew but if she had to guess, he didn't know she was pregnant because if he did, he wouldn't have been so mild-mannered.

"What you mean dad?" Mia asked suspiciously.

"I don't know. Have you gotten your final report card yet? Have you been working at one of the daycares? Anything! Talk to your daddy."

Mia noticed the look in her dad's eyes and knew exactly what that look was. It was the look of love. Tim just wanted to talk. He simply wanted father and daughter time which was typical of Tim. His love for Mia was like most active fathers were with their daughters. Mia was more than his only child. She was his world!

"I am still waiting on my report card. I am hoping I have all A's."

"Why wouldn't you? Are you worried that Mr. Rios will give you a B in Spanish?"

"Kind of." Mia shrugged. "Mr. Rios be tripping, Dad. He rarely gives A's as final grades no matter how well you did on his exams."

"I tell you what. If you don't have an A but you did your best, I will be happy. All I ask is that you do your best. So what else is going on?"

"I haven't been working at the daycares, lately. Grandma Rose hasn't accepted my application."

"That grandmother of yours is something else. She makes you apply ever summer only to hire you after the interview. She is truly something."

"She might not give me the job anyway," Mia mumbled.

"What you say?"

"Huh? Nothing. You know how Grandma Rose is. She does stuff on her time."

"True. But last summer you saved over a thousand dollars from working the daycares. That's not a job you turn down so easily. Plus, it looks good on your resume. Don't you want to be a Pediatric Nurse when you get older?"

Tim always preached the importance of making today count. As much money that he spent on tuition and extracurricular activities, he was making sure Mia was able to compete with anyone who had better access to education than she had.

"You're right, Dad. I do need to stay focus. Plus, when you're buying my first car, I can give you all the money I saved to make sure it's a brand new Mustang."

"I'll be glad to take your money sweetie. Now let's get you to Sky's before you miss all the fun," Tim said mockingly.

Mia smiled.

On their ride to Sky's, Tim put in a Johnny Taylor's cd and played his favorite song. He looked over at Mia who was riding shotgun in his brand new

2005 black Chevrolet Silverado with the word GANGSTA in bold letters on his tag. As if on cue, Mia looked over at Tim and in unison they sang. The tunes of Johnny Taylor matched with Tim's and Mia's vocals echoed throughout the speakers. Mia basked in the moment. With all that's going on and the secrets, Mia needed her father close. She needed to feel protected and she wanted things to feel normal.

Tim turned the radio down and said, "When you were little, I jammed this so much and look at you now. You know this song word for word."

"Dad, this song is as old as you are. Everybody knows this song." Mia chuckled.

"And everybody who does knows good music," he said as he snapped to the beat.

"I love you, Daddy."

"Aww. I love you too baby girl."

As they pulled into Sky's apartment complex, Tim noticed a group of young girls walking to the apartment's pool. He shook his head in disbelief.

"Now that don't make no sense. Look how these girls are dressing. They barely have on any clothes. I am so glad Sky doesn't act like these girls in her neighborhood. You definitely wouldn't be allowed over here, if she was."

"Dad. You're being judgmental. For one, they're headed to the pool and two, what do you suggest they wear?"

"I suggest they dress their age. Where are their parents? I sure do hope Pam isn't letting you and Sky dress like that to no pool. I'll be damned if you wore anything like what those girls have on."

Umph, poor daddy. You have no idea, Mia thought. "Okay, okay. Give me kiss so I can go. I'll call when you can pick me up tomorrow," Mia said, as she hurriedly kissed her Tim's cheek before exiting his truck.

Mia and Sky sat licking a popsicle on Sky's apartment stairwell. Sky lived with her mother and three sisters. They shared a three-bedroom apartment that was clearly overcrowded for a house full of estrogen. Sky rarely got along with her siblings. They spent most of their time avoiding each other and bickering about the smallest of things.

It was 95 degrees outside and there was no shade to be found. So many people were outside that no one seemed to care about the scorching heat. A group of boys was gambling, playing dice at the end of the staircase adjacent to the one Mia and Sky were sitting on.

Sky had her radio outside and Hot 97.7 was playing all the hot jams. Sky stopped licking her popsicle and said, "Bitch what's the tea?"

Mia gave Sky a crooked stare as if she was annoyed.

"Trick I know you and you holding back. So, what's up. We haven't talked in days and every time I hit you up, you got your mom blocking my calls. It can't be something I did because you wouldn't be over here," Sky said with concern.

Mia knew it was time to reveal her secret. It wasn't like she was ashamed to tell Sky. Sky was her girl. She was more so scared of saying it out loud because that made it her reality. Mia got up to throw her popsicle stick over the stair rail before spilling it all. She took a long deep breath and said, "I'm pregnant."

Sky looked at Mia with confusion. She then flipped her long box braids over her shoulder, as if they were blocking her hearing.

"Come again, say what?"

"Chick you heard correctly; I'm about four weeks."

"No way. I just can't believe it. I thought you and Drew were using protection? I didn't think you would get caught up like that. So, what are you going to do?"

"I'm not sure. I believe my grandma and ma are going to make me have an abortion," Mia said with sadness.

"Damn, this is better than a marathon of The Young and the Restless."

"Sky, how can you joke at a time like this?"

"My bad. I've never seen you like this. Normally we joke our way through everything, but I don't know how to respond to this type of news."

Sky was doing what they normally did. They rarely ever took anything seriously. When Sky's mother went missing for about three days, Sky called Mia in the same joking tone. Only to later find out that her mother had spent several nights at the casino and neglected to call and tell her children. This was how they seemed to cope with things.

"Mia, you know my story. You know how my dad isn't around and not to say I wish he was, but I do know how it feels to grow up with a distant father. Maybe that's why I do the shit I do. Ya know? If had a dad who was around and a mother to stay at home, I wouldn't be out for self. I know why I am the way I am but, you, I don't get you. Why?"

"Why, what?"

"Why do you do this shit. All the shit we do! Why?"

"I don't really have a perfect answer. My life isn't perfect but if I could make it simple for you, I just do it. I can't explain it. It's like having access to a drug that you never get to touch. I guess you can say that the stuff we do is my drug," Mia said matter-of-factly. There was a long pause. Neither of them knew what to say. The topic was like an open wound and nobody wanted to dress it. So they didn't.

"How about, we see if I can get the keys to my ma's car and we go ridding," Sky said, as this always seemed to fix their problems.

Mia, hoping to shake the funk she was in, quickly nodded in agreeance.

Sky drove her mother's car to Lake Hico. Lake Hico was a park on the north side of the city where a lot of the older crowd hung out. Sky used to go there often with her older sister last summer and the park was always jumping. From local dope boys, fast sassy girls, up and coming rappers, b-ball crews, and car clubs, everybody who had nothing to do on Saturdays hung out there. It was definitely the place to be.

"Dang Sky this park is the shit!" Mia said in excitement, as Sky found a park on the side of the street. It was so many people out that there was nowhere to park on the actual park site. Mia and Sky had to walk to get close to the action. Mia, still wearing her blue and white striped dress, decided to tie her dress in a knot around the ankle to show off her ankle bracelet.

Sky fitted right in with the scene. Sky with her smooth dark skin complexion let her long jet-black braids flow. She stood 5'4 wearing a fitted blue jean skirt that barely stopped over her butt, a pink halter top that was cut off at the midriff, and stylish studded thong flip flops she copped at Forever 21. On her face, she wore some knock off Gucci shades, face flawless with Mac makeup, and light lip gloss to complement her lips. Sky was stunning. She looked every bit of 18 and most compared her to a sassier version of Gabriel Union. While Sky looked mature, Mia looked innocent yet beautiful.

As they walked through the park, they heard different types of rap music blaring from car speakers. Some were playing the newest Lil'Boosie, some were playing their own mixtapes, and some were playing New Orleans bounce music.

The sun was beginning to settle, and the light breeze made everyone feel chill. No one appeared to be beefing just cool vibes. Mia and Sky found a place amongst a crew of rappers and local dealers to hangout. The crew was standing around drinking and smoking. Sky particularly picked this spot due to the way the crew handled themselves. Sky knew the guys who were flashy didn't have money and the guys who were the loudest were the brokest. The way this crew looked said they were the crew to mingle with. Their gold chains were small, some even had gold teeth, but they weren't show-boating and trying to out stunt the next crew. Sky knew if she and Mia played their cards right, they'll be amongst the chosen.

"Aye little mama, ya'll want a wine cooler?" A dark skin guy with dreads asked them.

"Sure," Sky said without hesitation.

He passed Mia two green apple Smirnoff's. "What's yo' name lil' mama?" the guy said nodding at Sky.

"Sky," she said as she passed Mia a Smirnoff.

"Oh, that's different. My name is Will but people who know me call me Dub."

"Nice to meet you, Will. I'm Sky and this is my girl, Mia."

Dub began to chuckle.

"What's funny?" Sky asked.

"Nothing. It's just I told you my name was Dub but you called me Will. I find that interesting that's all."

"Well, Will," Sky said as she leaned on the bench. "You also said people who know you call you Dub, and I don't know you," she said with sass.

"Yet!"

"Excuse me?"

"I said you don't know me, yet. But I have a good feeling you will very soon," Dub said as he blew out the smoke from his weed his friend had just passed him. Sky and Dub locked eyes. "Come err and let me rap with you," Dub called out to Sky.

"Nah, didn't your mama teach you some manners? A lady is always approached never hollered at." This time they both laughed. Dub walked over to where Mia and Sky were standing and grabbed Sky's hand, as they began to walk and talk.

This bitch is always leaving me to fend for myself, Mia thought as she sat on the bench feeling her Smirnoff kick in. Mia nor Sky were drinkers. They made a pack to never do drugs and if they drunk, it would only be something light. Nothing that would cloud their judgment if they ever were in a sticky situation.

Mia didn't even think about her pregnancy. She sipped her drink until it was gone, and she had a nice little buzz.

Mia noticed this up and coming rapper name, Rossi. Mia had seen him a couple of times. One time she was in the mall with her mother and he was in the shoe store. Another time, Rossi had come to the school to judge the school's talent show. Both times she was star struck.

Rossi was fine! Mia couldn't stop admiring his strapping physique in the fitted white muscle shirt he had on, and the way his mahogany skin shimmered under the sunset. *Mmm!* Mia thought.

Rossi had on a pair of stylish khaki cargo shorts, with a pair of black and red Jordan 7s. His tattooed arms were glistening in sweat and around his neck he wore a simple Cuban link chain with a diamond-encrusted cross. He had just finished a game of basketball and the sweat just seemed to glisten off his forehead.

Rossi was the definition of what Mia envisioned a thug to look like. Well-groomed, humorous, and everyone loved him. She couldn't stop drooling at the sight of him. She often fantasized about being his girl. She pictured herself riding in his 2005 Silver Chevy Camaro, sitting in the passenger seat, being his woman, and all the other bum bitches chasing after her man. But she knew Rossi was only probably checking for older maybe college type girls. She knew she wasn't even on his radar. Like her mother always said, "You catch a man with patience and not your mouth." All she had to do was be at the right place at the right time and Rossi would be hers.

Chapter 4

*M*ia hadn't spoken to Drew in a week. He had been blowing her cellphone up. She honestly didn't know what to say to him. To make matters worse, Drew's cousin saw Mia at Lake Hico and had the nerve to call himself telling Drew.

> "Mia. Like what the fuck ma. You all at Lake Hico and shit. You trying to play me or something? Hit me back, ma."

Mia rolled her eyes as she listened to the voicemail. "Yea, I got this nigga checking for me now but wasn't he the one who didn't want a girlfriend? Tuh! Niggas," Mia mumbled. She knew it was time to tell Drew that she was pregnant.

Being that the week was so crazy she never thought about how it would affect him, too. She didn't know if she cared. It seemed like being pregnant made Mia colder because a week prior she wouldn't dare go a day without talking to Drew. She decided to give Drew a call and see if he could get a ride to her house. Today, her mother was helping Grandma Rose at the daycare and her father was states away delivering goods in Texas. There was no other time that was more perfect than today.

Mia quickly dialed the number. Drew answered on the first ring. "Sup," he said coldly. Mia looked at the phone with a crooked neck. *No, he didn't*, she thought. Mia heard loud noises in the background, and it sounded like Drew was hanging with Troy, and knowing them, they were up to something.

"Umm, I was calling you to see... to see if you could get a ride to my house," Mia stuttered.

"Oh, so you ain't at Lake Hico which ya girl right now. You want to call a nigga back and shit." Drew sounded salty and to Mia, he sounded like he cared. She kind of felt bad about how she had been ignoring him. And a part of her felt like he didn't deserve it. Partly because he was her unborn child's father.

"Look. I'm inviting you over because we need to talk. A lot has been going on and I rather not say it over the phone. Can you come over or not?" Mia said getting straight to the point.

"Aye lame ass nigga, you gonna play or you gonna let me keep tearing in that ass!" Troy said loudly in the background.

Mia immediately knew they were playing basketball on Troy's brother's PlayStation. "Damn nigga I'm coming give me a minute," Drew said barely taking his mouth off the phone.

"Hello! Hello! Heeellllllooo!" Mia yelled, becoming more irritable by the second.

"A'ight, A'ight, I am going to get Troy to bring me over there. I'll be there in a second." Without further explanation, he hung up. Mia knew it would take them thirty minutes to drive from Troy's place to Mia's subdivision, so it would be a while before he arrived. That's if they didn't decide to finish their game of NBA 2K6, first.

Mia lived in a suburban neighborhood right outside of Jackson. Mia's parents worked hard to distance Mia from the crime rate that was increasing in the local city. The city's crime was becoming so bad that they often considered themselves blessed to be away from such violence. No matter what time of day you turned on the news, you would always see some headline about gun violence, drugs, or robbery happening in Jackson, MS.

Mia attended a private school called Christian Academy. She hated it there. She wanted to attend public school with Sky to show them prep bitches, how to have fun. Her parents wouldn't dare let her go to school with her bestie. Mia started thinking about when she first met her best friend.

Sky and Mia met on a field trip. Sky's school was volunteering at an MLK parade that Mia's school attended. Sky was working the concession stand when Mia walked up. Sky overhead some girls teasing Mia about wearing glasses. "Mia, what's taking you so long to order? Can't you see the whole menu with those thick glasses you got on?" two of Christian Academy's notorious bullies stated. Sarah and Amber were known for teasing kids. No matter how you looked or what you had on, they always found something negative to say. But, one thing about Mia, she wasn't insecure, and she wasn't no one's pushover. If Grandma Rose taught her anything, it was always to stand up for herself.

Mia slowly turned around, as if time was waiting on her and said, "Sarah and Amber while you up here waiting at the concession stand, I overheard Ms. Gale telling the other teachers that ya'll daddies couldn't afford tuition this month. You might want to give your "bankrupt daddies" a call to make sure you can even afford what's at the concession stand," Mia exclaimed using air quotes to solidify her stance.

Everyone burst out into laughter. The whole line was in tears. No one liked Sarah or Amber and they couldn't wait until someone put them in their place. Mia stood looking them both square in their eyes as if she was saying "Try me". Neither girl said a word and exited the line as quickly as they came.

"Dang girl you were cold with them stuck up bitches!" Sky said jumping up and down in excitement. "My name is Sky. What's yours?"

"I'm Tamia, but I go by Mia."

"You're my type of chick," Sky said. "I can get down with you. You're not like them other prep bitches who been coming up here all rude and shit. You're cool." And, from that moment, at the age of ten, they've been friends ever since.

Mia couldn't do anything but laugh thinking about how she and Sky met. It was like they clicked instantly and ever since then they have been best friends. They've been inseparable, and you would rarely see one without the other. Although they attended different schools and lived in different neighborhoods, they always made time to see each other; so much so, Mia's parents and Sky's mother have trusted them to spend unsupervised time together. Some would say that they had too much "trust" with their parents. No matter how the story was told, truth be told, they loved it!

Mia heard a strong knock at the door. She also heard loud music blaring from what sounded like a car speaker. She instantly knew it was Drew and Troy. *What kinda fools play loud music in a quiet neighborhood like this? Fools,* she thought to herself. Mia wanted to look casual yet seductive. She decided to wear black biker shorts with a loose fitted t-shirt. She knew the biker shorts would give her ass the extra glance from Drew. When she opened the door, Drew was standing there looking annoyed.

"What's wrong with you?" Mia asked as she stepped to the side to let him in.

Drew simply walked past her without saying a word. The arch in his brow told Mia all she needed to know. He walked straight to the couch and sat down casually. Drew began looking around Mia's house. He had never been inside and was taken back by how well decorated it was. He knew Mia was a prep girl, but he had no clue how she was living. The way Mia acted when she was in the hood didn't match the way she lived.

"Damn ma, this some Huxtable type shit," Drew stated with one leg crossed over his knee and both arms propped on top of the couch. Mia gave Drew a blank stare. Drew must've just gotten his braids done because they were extra fresh. The scalp was still tight. He had on a Kobe Bryant Lakers number 8 jersey with blue jeans, Laker socks, and a pair of white Air Force Ones. As she stared at him, he purposefully flashed her a smile.

"What you smiling at?" Mia said asked while rolling her eyes with her arms crossed, as she stood in the middle of the living room.

"Come err," Drew seductively patted the seat next to him.

"Unt uh. I am not fucking with you."

"Stop acting like you didn't miss me. You got me way out here in this damn police ass town only to act funny with a nigga. You better come show me love, with them short ass shorts on. I know you wore them for me."

"Oh, so you checking for me now?"

"Mia, I'm always checking for you," Drew said, matter-of-factly.

"Well. Well, I got something I want to talk to you about. You might not after I tell you this."

Mia walked over to Drew looking like she was about to drop a bomb. She was so nervous. Although she had replayed the scenario over and over in her mind, she wasn't prepared for the anxiety to be accompanied with it. She sat on the couch and turned to face him.

"Drew. I don't even know what to say. If you never want to talk to me again, I completely understand."

"Yo. Wassup? Come on with the spill so I can know what's up. You been playing me to the left for the past week. That ain't cool, yo."

"I know and I'm sorry. I just been wanting to tell you." There was a pause. Mia held her head down as if the words wouldn't roll off her tongue. They were right in her thoughts, but it just didn't seem to come out. Drew lifted Mia's head by her chin and prompted her to look him square in the eyes. Whatever she was about to say, he wanted her to be a woman about it.

"I'm pregnant!" Mia exclaimed.

"You what?!? DAAMMMMNNN, MA!"

"I know. I know what you're thinking."

"Mia, I swear to God. I didn't think you were about to say you pregnant. I told Troy on the way over here if you told me you were fucking another nigga, it was about to be some murder shit out here."

"Fucking another nigga?" Mia angrily questioned. She folded her arms and waited for a reply. Before he could say anything, she kept talking. "I am so wrapped around your braids that I don't even have time to fuck somebody else."

Mia was hurt that Drew would even think that. She expected him to flip his lid but had no idea that would come out his mouth. Drew was the only person Mia was sleeping with. Hell, he was her first. For him to think she was giving it up to other dudes made her livid. She no longer wanted to talk about the pregnancy, she wanted to address his real thoughts. The thoughts of her being some type of hoe were the conversation she wanted to have. Mia got up and began to pace the floor. She couldn't seem to think while sitting down. She looked over at Drew who was looking at her like she was the crazy one.

"So you pregnant?" Drew asked.

"Yea," Mia said as she began to slow her pace down.

"Yo, so what does this mean? What did your parents say?"

"My dad doesn't know. My grandma and mom are making me have an abortion. Strange thing is, they told me as if I have no choice."

"Do you want a baby?"

Mia completely stopped pacing and thought about it. She didn't know what she wanted. Apart of her wanted to live her life and continue hanging with Sky and not worry about bringing a baby along. But another side of her wanted to see what life would be like as a mom.

"I don't know. I hadn't thought about it. What do you want?" Now it was Drew's turn to be in the hot seat. Mia didn't know how Drew would respond but she was ready to pop off if he said anything she didn't like.

"I mean. This shit is so unexpected. I mean you got to think about this shit Mia. You're fourteen and I am five years older than you. Shit could get real ugly for me. And don't get me wrong, I am not trying to make this about me because that's not the case. But whatever you decide, you still my girl."

Mia felt her heart melt. To see this side of Drew was not something she expected. Although she didn't know what he was going to say, she hadn't predicted him to be so caring. Drew got up and walked to stand in front of her. The more he looked at her, he could see the innocence within her. She was so fragile, and he didn't want to break her. He felt like it was his responsibility and anyway he could he wanted to protect her.

At this moment, Drew was vulnerable. All the player and smooth-talking he did with girls were out the window. He wanted Mia. He wanted to love her and treat her right. In some strange way, he knew this feeling wouldn't last long so he wanted to make sure he took full advantage.

Drew began rubbing Mia's belly. He felt the slight bulge that was forming. It made him feel things he hadn't felt before. It also made him horny. Drew had heard from the streets that girls who were pregnant had better sex and he wanted to find out for himself. Mia was the first girl he had sex with that was a virgin and she would be the first to give him a sample of what the insides felt like while pregnant. His penis grew in excitement. Drew started kissing her forehead repeatedly. Before they knew it, they were in a full-blown passionate kiss. Drew's kisses were so soft and tender. Mia wanted Drew in the worst way. Her body began to tense up and her mind began to forget the issue at hand. She wanted Drew to take her to her room and make her call him daddy. And that's exactly what Drew had on his mind.

Drew picked Mia up and wrapped her legs around his waist. Drew kissed her sloppily on her neck, cheeks, and lips. She didn't care that he was sucking so hard that he could leave a hickey. She was already in hot water. What's the worst that could happen?

Drew gently laid Mia down on her bed. This time he wanted to see her naked. He slipped her shirt over her head and with one hand unsnapped her bra.

Her nipples were already erect. While he began sliding her shorts off, he licked and sucked on her nipples. Mia moaned in pleasure.

As many times that they've had sex, Drew had never taken her shirt off or even touched her breast. The feeling felt foreign to her, but it felt like heaven. Once her shorts were off, he slowly and tenderly kissed her stomach. He gently nibbled the side of her stomach to make her moan louder.

"*Oooo.* Baby, what are you doing to me," Mia moaned loudly. Her eyes began to roll to the back of her head.

Drew didn't stop there. He positioned himself were Mia's legs were up in the air and his head was between her legs. "Hold up baby. What are you doing?"

Drew had never given Mia oral before. Neither of them had pleased each other on this level. However, Drew was very skilled in this area. Drew looked at oral sex as a task you do with someone you trusted and loved. At the moment, he felt both for Mia. Drew kissed Mia's inner thigh and she immediately jumped. "Just relax baby. Do you trust me?"

Tight-lipped, she said, "*Mmmhmm.*"

He attempted again. This time he added tongue. He worked his way from her left thigh to the right. Slowly letting his warm tongue touch her skin. Once he felt she was all worked up, he opened her lips and began licking on her clit. Mia moaned so loudly that

46

Drew thought the neighbors heard her. He didn't stop. His warm long tongue worked her clitoris like a skilled scientist. Mia tasted so good to him. He purposely let the juices run down his chin just to lick it off. Mia was moaning and groaning and sliding up the bed to run from Drew. She had no clue what had gotten over him, but she loved every second.

"Ohh baby I'm about to come daddy."

With the sound of Mia calling him daddy, he sent Drew over the edge. He quickly got up and began kissing her. He gently slides his rock-hard penis inside of her slippery vagina. Mia tightened her legs and wrapped them around Drew.

"Damn Mia, I love you," Drew stated truthfully. "Come with me, Mia."

Drew began to pump faster and faster and Mia yelped in pleasure. Her body couldn't take any more as she reached her peek so did Drew. Before either of them knew, they were climaxing together. Drew rolled over and let Mia lie on his chest. Neither of them said a word. Drew rubbed her hair while Mia listened to his steady heartbeat. The moment felt so perfect. Nothing mattered and if the moment never happened again, they would remember this one.

Chapter 5

Mia dreadfully woke up the next morning. Today was the day she was not prepared for. She and Drew had spent most of the previous day trying to bask in the moment and not talk about the day to come. However, they both decided that going along with the abortion was the best thing to do. They knew that neither of them was prepared to be parents and neither of them wanted to deal with the level of stress that announcing their relationship would cause. It seemed selfish, to both of them, to raise a child under such conditions. Mia desperately wanted more time to be pregnant. Strangely, she wanted to know what it felt like to carry a baby. She wanted to make her own rules and do what she pleased without dealing with the repercussions from her parents and Grandma Rose. She didn't know where this thing she had with Drew would take them but at this moment she just wanted to pretend. Pretending felt normal. It felt liberating.

"Mia what are you doing? Are you ready?" Mrs. Jackson screamed from her bedroom. And just like that reality set back in.

After finding out about Mia's pregnancy, Mrs. Jackson had been clocking her more and more lately. If Mia was in the shower too long, she would open the door without knocking just to check on her. If Mia had a phone call, she would tell them Mia couldn't talk. If Mia wanted to go outside for fresh air, Mia had to stay in the front yard where Mrs. Jackson could see her. The only time Mia was able to escape was when Tim was home. Because Mrs. Jackson was keeping Mia's pregnancy a secret, she maintained normalcy when Tim was around. Mia noticed and enjoyed every moment of her freedom. She talked on the phone, asked her dad to take her to see Sky, and did everything she wanted to do. While Mrs. Jackson didn't like it, she held a tight lip and didn't stop it. She too felt that once the procedure was over that everything would go back to normal again. Mrs. Jackson wasn't naive. She knew what young girls did and how they acted when they weren't under direct supervision. But to her, Mia was her child and if raised right then she could prevent things from happening. She believed that if she prevented Mia from seeing the world then she would eventually find a way to see it. By letting Mia learn from her mistakes would teach her how to make better decisions, especially if she was burned the first time.

Only if Mrs. Jackson knew.

Mia walked out of her room in a slow drag with a black Nike sweatsuit on, rocking a pair of black Nike Airmax, with the hood over her head. She wanted to look how she felt. Empty!

"Pick your face up and get in the car. Your grandmother is going to meet us there."

Mia noticed her mother's tone was rather cold and piercing. It wasn't like her to exude such coldness. She was fair toned and very soft-spoken. Mia never thought about how all this made her feel. So wrapped in her feelings, it's been all about Mia. She didn't consider how her mother felt about her fourteen-year-old daughter being pregnant.

Like deja vu, Mia and her mother rode in complete silence. While both of them were in deep thought, the radio announced:

"GET READY! GET READY! The livest concert this summer you will ever see is coming to the coliseum near you. Starring Young Jeezy, T.I., Lil' Boosie, and The Trill Fam with opening acts from Rossi, Da Don, and Parkway Beats. It's going down! Tickets are now on sale and are selling fast. You don't want to miss it. And you heard it here first at 99 Jams WJMI."

Mia perked up at the radio advertisement. Not only were her favorites T.I. and Young Jeezy performing but Rossi was blessing the stage. If she knew one thing, she and Sky were there. No matter the cost, they were their backstage rubbing shoulders with celebs. *This might work out in my favor after all*, Mia thought. Mia couldn't wait to call Sky and formulate their master plan. The summer was still young, and she refused to let this incident ruin what was left of it.

As they arrived at the clinic, there were protestors outside screaming and chanting. Mia read their signs, "Abortion is murder. Save the heartbeat!" Mrs. Jackson noticed Mia's face flush.

"When we get out, ignore them and keep walking," Mrs. Jackson stated.

Mia saw so many women and even men standing on the corner of the clinic. They all held different signs but there was one man who was reading bible verses.

"Psalm 127 verse 3 through 5 reads, 'Children are a heritage from the LORD, offspring a reward from him. Like arrows in the hands of a warrior are children born in one's youth. Blessed is the man whose quiver is full of them. They will not be put to shame when they contend with their opponents in court.'"

Scripture after scripture he read. Never taking a moment to breathe, he was relentless with his efforts.

Mia and her mother got out of the car. Mia felt someone grab her arm. She jumped in fear. Mia turned around and looked into the eyes of an older white woman.

"I see it in your eyes. You don't have to do this. It's your body and the Lord forgives you," the woman confessed as she held Mia's wrist tightly. The woman stares were menacing. Mrs. Jackson noticed the holdup and turned to grab Mia. "SHE'S JUST A CHILD!" The lady screamed while watching them walk away.

Once inside, Mia noticed there was a mixture of girls and women there. Women of all ages and sizes. Some alone, some accompanied by what looked to be their partner, and some with upset parents. The small clinic felt full but the life in the waiting room felt empty.

"Go sit down while I sign you in," Mrs. Jackson said as she pointed Mia to her seat.

When Mia turned around, she saw Grandma Rose sitting inconspicuously. She was adjacent to the receptionist window but far from the door. She too appeared to be hiding. Sitting there with her calm and reserved demeanor, Grandma Rose stood out like a sore thumb. Her attire looked as if she just left Saks' dressing room. She wore a Louis Vuitton pinstripe suit with a matching handbag. Her Louis Vuitton loafers accompanied her wardrobe by giving it a splash of color. Anyone who knew designers knew what brand Grandma Rose was wearing because of the LV stitching. She loved the flashy look. She always kept it expensive and tasteful.

Mia sat next to Grandma Rose. She normally greeted her with a kiss to the cheek or a cheerful, "Hey Grandma!" but at this moment, neither felt befitting.

"Because you're mad or in your feelings as you say, you still speak," Grandma Rose harshly stated.

Grandma Rose, having three children at a young age, knew what Mia felt. She didn't approve of Mia having sex but around this age, she was pregnant with her first son. The only difference is, immediately afterward, Grandma Rose got married. It didn't seem like there were no other options for her. If she was having children, she was going to marry the child's father. Thankfully for her, she and Morris were in love. Her only goal now was to protect Mia from ruining her promising future. She wanted so much for Mia. Mia was her eldest grandchild and her most prized possession. She had this saying, "I can verify that you are my grandchild because you came from my daughter. Now the others, they may or may not be my grandchildren because they came from my sons." Grandma Rose was vocal and never filtered. She would either talk her way out of it or pay her way out. Simple!

Mia spoke dryly and kept her head turned so she wouldn't feel the stare from Grandma Rose.

"Mia, look at me," Grandma Rose said more sternly.

"I love you and I hope you love yourself just as much to know that you have so much life to live. This boy, whoever he is, is not worth your future. You might be having fun and thinking that your actions don't have repercussions, well they do. Look where we are. Look at the girls around you. You are so blessed and loved, and you should never take that for granted. You can tell me anything. I will always be by your side. I might not approve, and I may even fuss but just know I am always by your side," Grandma Rose said sincerely. Mia was stunned and before she could respond, her number was called.

"Number 96708," the nursing assistant called.

Mia hugged both her mother and grandmother before following the young black nurse behind the door that separated the waiting room and examination rooms.

Mia took a deep breath and reminded herself that everything was going to be okay.

The nurse handed her a gown and said, "Here, take this. Put your clothes in the locker and once you are done, come back out and sit right along this wall. Once one person gets up, you slide down until it's your turn. Any questions?"

"No."

The nurse wasn't rude, but you can tell she wasn't for the formalities or accommodating the women's feelings. Mia changed and came out to sit where the nurse had told her. There were about six people in front of her and the line seemed to move quickly. She sat shaking her legs and blankly stared at the floor. She wondered how many girls the doctor saw a day.

"Are you nervous?"

"Huh?" Mia said as she looked up.

"I asked if you're nervous," the girl to her left said.

"Yea, kinda."

"Don't be. This is my third time. It goes by quickly. I'm Justice by the way."

"Mia," she replied while shaking Justice's hand. "Why is this your 3rd time?" Mia asked, sounding so naive.

"Girl, when you get pregnant, you quickly realize that the man you thought is the one is not. Plus my lifestyle doesn't allow me to bring a child into the mix."

"What do you do for a living?"

"I am a dancer. I often travel from Atlanta or Miami to dance."

"You mean like a stripper?"

Justice laughed. "You're so cute. How old are you?"

"Fourteen," Mia said wondering if she said something wrong.

"Yes, Mia. Like a stripper," Justice continued to lightly laugh.

As Mia and Justice continued to talk, the line continued to move and before they both knew it, it was Justice's turn.

"It was good to meet you, Mia. I hate it was under this circumstance but what's your locker number? I will slip my number in it."

"It's locker number four."

"Once you heal up. Give me a call." Justice gave Mia a wink and walked into the examining room.

Mia thought Justice was so nice and brave for going through this for the third time. She was grateful that Justice helped her take her mind off the anxiety she was feeling. She planned to call Justice when this was all over and hoped she remembered her.

"Next!" Someone called from the small room. Mia slowly got up. It was now her turn. When Mia sat down, her eyes quickly scanned the room. The room was small and the chipped paint with no pictures made the room feel lonely. Abandoned, even.

"Hey, I'm nurse Shay, and I'm going to take your vitals. Once we are done, you will walk down to examining room eight. There you will meet the anesthesiologist to be prepped for your procedure."

Mia just nodded in agreement to signify she understood.

Nurse Shay rolled the blood pressure machine over in front of Mia. She took Mia's blood pressure and put the thermometer in her mouth to check her temperature. Once she was done, she asked Mia to stand on the scale to get her weight.

"Okay, Ms. Tamia. We are all done here. Remember you are going to room eight and someone will meet you there."

Mia made her way to room eight. She passed a few girls who were now waiting along the wall she was once on. It was like they were moving patients like a track meet. When one moved, another was up next.

Mia entered room eight to see a man standing while looking at the computer screen. Without turning to greet Mia, he said, "Come on in and lie down on the examining table. Once you have done so, put your feet on the stirrups."

Mia did as she was instructed. Her heart was beating a million miles per hour. She wished her mother or Grandma Rose could be back here with her, but the rules prohibited others to be present. Nurse Shay walked in and greeted doctor Reese.

"Tamia, it's me, Nurse Shay, and I will be monitoring your baby. Would you like to hear the heartbeat?"

Mia was taken back by Nurse Shay's question. Why would she ask her that knowing what was about to happen? Not knowing it was standard protocol Mia tensed up. She began to question everything. Feeling trapped, Mia asked, "Can I have some water?"

"Unfortunately, you cannot have any food or drinks until your procedure is over. I'm sorry."

Mia wanted to cry. The question still lingered. Did she want to hear her baby's heartbeat?

With a slight stutter and tremble of the lip, Mia said, "Yyyee… yes."

Nurse Shay gently lifted the gown and added what appeared to be lube on Mia's stomach. It was cold and had a tingling sensation. Nurse Shay pressed a few keys on the monitor and rubbed the doppler back and forth across the lube that was on Mia's stomach until she found a beat.

THUMP. THUMP. THUMP.

For the first time, Mia heard her baby's strong and sturdy heartbeat. With a lump in her chest, Mia softly said, "Turn it off please." Mia felt queasy and lightheaded. She felt anxious and just wanted to get up and run full force for the door. She didn't want to be here. She wanted the abortion, but the pressure of all the tests and probing was too much. This is not what she predicted. Nurse Shay looked at Mia and understood her facial expression. She had seen so many with the same look on their faces. Mia's head was turned towards the wall away from the doctor and nurse. She didn't want them to see the defeat in her eyes. She starred at the black and white picture on the wall. It was a picture of a lake. She felt connected with the picture. She too felt colorless.

Dr. Reese began to explain to Mia that he was about to run an IV in her hand that would sedate her. He explained that she would be put to sleep temporarily for the procedure and when she woke up, the procedure would be over, and she would be in the recovery room. He asked her to nod if she understood. With her head still turned facing the colorless picture on the wall, Mia slowly nodded as tears fell from the crease of her eyes. "Great. I now want you to count backwards from ten."

Mia saw the doctor who was going to do her procedure walk into the room. She didn't get a good look at her due to the mask she had around her mouth, cap overhead, and full scrub on. All Mia could see were her restless eyes. Mia began to feel the medicine in her throat. It made its way to her tongue buds and it tasted strong; like a taste that couldn't be described. She began counting, "Ten, nine, eight, seven, six...."

Mia was awakened by another unfamiliar face.

"Would you like some ice chips?"

Mia tried to clear her throat. It felt like she had several cotton balls stuck in her throat. Her mouth was so dry that she could barely swallow. As she took the ice chips, she observed her surroundings. She was sitting in a lazy boy recliner with a blanket over her. She noticed Justice who gave her a friendly thumbs up. Mia tried to smile but her mouth wouldn't form the simplest act. She was given some medicine to take and was told to take them every seven hours until all the pills were gone. Mia was then directed to get her clothes out of her locker and to put one of the pads in the restroom in her panties before she completely dressed.

As she exited the restroom, the lady helped her onto the wheelchair and escorted her through the waiting room and out the front door. Mrs. Jackson was waiting for her with the car running. Mia was transferred from the wheelchair to the car, and the nurse handed Mrs. Jackson Mia's discharge paperwork. Mia made eye contact with Grandma Rose who was sitting parallel in her car. Grandma Rose winked at Mia and Mia winked back. This gesture made Mia feel relieved. It showed Mia that there was no love loss with Grandma Rose, and she had Mia's back. Mia got comfortable, as much she could, in her seat, and prepared for her ride home.

Chapter 6

For the past three days, Mia had been lying in bed. She would only leave her room to change her pad and to get the food that her mother refused to bring to her room. She didn't want to do anything else. That included showering, responding to Sky's and Drew's text messages, or to find the remote to the TV. Her TV had been on Lifetime Movie Network for the past three days because it matched her mood. All the drama and suspense were aligned with her internal emotions. Noticing a change in Mia, Tim decided to check on her. Tim knocked on the door with a light knock. "Baby girl can I come in?"

She wanted to say, "No leave me alone," but she knew her father didn't deserve that. "Yes, Dad. Come in."

Tim walked in and sat on the ottoman at the end of Mia's bed. He scanned the room and instantly smelled the stench.

"Eww, what's that smell? Mia this room is a mess and that is not like you. You used to always keep your room clean. What's going on?"

Mia knew her father was right. She felt guilty for letting her outside match her inside. The smell Tim smelt was Mia's body odor. She hadn't bathed in days and being that she was bleeding intensified the smell. She smelled horrible and she didn't care.

"I don't know, Dad. I guess I am depressed because we aren't going on our annual summer vacation this year. I always look forward to them and knowing we aren't going makes me sad," Mia said with her head hung low while speaking in a childlike tone. Tim instantly felt guilty. The reason they weren't going on their annual summer vacation was because he had accepted a part-time job with another trucking company. He was already in a managerial position at his current job but had been saving up to buy Mrs. Jackson a new ring for their 15th anniversary.

The one she was currently wearing was gifted to them by Grandma Rose and he no longer wanted her to wear that one. He felt like the more money and things Grandma Rose gifted them, the more she inserted herself into their family affairs. He wanted to be the only head of his household and didn't need his mother-in-law making decisions in his house. Neither Mia or Mrs. Jackson knew why their annual trip was canceled but they weren't too happy with the lack of reasons behind it. However, Tim had no clue it was affecting Mia like this, so he thought.

"Baby girl, I am so sorry. I promise I will make it up to you and your mother. I didn't know you felt like this. What can daddy do to make things right?"

Like music to her ears, Mia's brain started working a thousand times over. She knew her father's soft spot and the biggest one he had was the one for his baby girl.

"Well... Since you mentioned it, I did want to go to the concert that's happening this weekend," Mia said as she held her head down and rubbed her hands across the pillow that was in her lap.

"Have you asked your mom about it?"

"No, because lately, she hasn't been letting me do anything. It seems like she is mad at me like I am the reason we are not going on the trip."

"It sounds like things have been pretty tense around here while I am away. We might need a family outing day. Just the three of us."

"I mean that's fine. I like spending time with you daddy, but I do want to go to the concert. All of my classmates are going, and I don't want to be the only one left out."

Mia planted the seed. Because she attended a predominately white private school, it always appeared like the black students were out of place if they didn't attend certain events or didn't look a certain way. Mia would often complain about how her peers acted towards her when she wouldn't wear a certain brand of clothing or if there was an event at school that she didn't attend. She usually told her parents because she wanted to go to public schools not because she had been teased.

In all honesty, the kids at her school liked Mia because she wasn't a follower. She made her trends and rules. And the outcast kids, who weren't allowed in the, what Mia called "uppity kids circle" respected her. And the "uppity kids" respected her too but they just kept their distance. She had the crazy black kid label amongst that group. And she was fine with that.

"Daddy, can you just buy my ticket and tell mom you're going to let me go?"

Tim began to scratch the bottom of his goatee. "I guess daddy can do that. Pull out your computer and let's order daddy's girl front row."

Mia instantly began to jump up and down and hugged Tim around his neck.

"Thank you, Daddy! Thank you, Daddy!" Mia said while repeatedly kissing him on his forehead. "Umm, Daddy."

"What now Mia?" Tim stated quizzically.

"Can you order Sky a ticket, too? I would hate for her to be in the back while all my other friends are in the front row with me. That wouldn't be fair."

"I mean, I don't see the problem in doing that. Book two front row tickets," Tim said in excitement.

Just seeing Mia light up made Tim's heart flutter. He only wanted Mia to be happy and he had just saved the day.

In Mia's mind, he just secured an event to the ride of her life. Not only was she front row, but she also had her bestie, Sky, right along for the ride. She couldn't be more ecstatic. All she wanted to do now was call Sky and plan their night.

"Can you do something for your daddy?"

"Yes, Daddy. Anything."

"Can you get in the shower?"
They both laughed.

———————◆•◆———————

Mia sat on the phone with Sky browsing the web for their outfits. Mia had gotten $150 from Drew to buy her an outfit for the concert. She was expecting to share some of it with Sky but, to Mia's surprise, Sky had already secured a full $200 from the guy she met at Lake Hico, Dub.

"Ain't no way he gave you $200. I don't even want to know what you had to do for it," Mia stated as she laid across her bed scrolling on her laptop with her headphones in.

"I didn't have to do shit. Girl, I met up with Dub as soon as you told me your daddy bought them tickets. He came over to my house and we sat in the parking lot a few complexes down from mine. We talked for about two hours until he had to go," Sky exclaimed.

"How did you get the $200 out of him?" Mia was all ears now.

"Damn trick. Let me finish. So we were sitting in his car, he asked me to roll up for him while he counted his money. I knew what he was trying to do but I acted like I wasn't fazed. He was trying to show off his money to see if I would look impressed. And of course, I didn't. I just sat there and rolled that blunt like I was pro. That nigga probably thought I was a smoker the way I rolled it up. I passed him the blunt and he started smoking it. I started giving him some sob story about how my mother's light bill had been due for a few weeks and it probably would be cut off soon. I had him right where I wanted him when he asked me, "How much is it?" I told him the light bill had gotten up to $400 after my mom had asked for so many extensions. Then I told him, we were only $200 short. You know what happened next," Sky said.

Mia sat up in her bed and leaned on the headboard. If she knew Sky, something juicy went down and she didn't want Sky to spare any details.

"Keep going. Girl what happened next?" Mia asked excitedly.

"At first he just rested his hand on my knee. When he noticed I didn't move it, he started casually rubbing his hand up and down my thigh. He started telling me how that was fucked up and yadda, yadda. Before I knew it, this nigga had his whole tongue down my throat. Girl I couldn't even breathe! All I am thinking is, *Sky, control the situation*. I told him I liked him and wanted to take things slow. I still wanted that money, so I knew I had to give up something. I pulled my left titty out of my bra and lifted my shirt so he could see my hard nipples. He started caressing it and quickly put the whole titty in his mouth. He was sucking and slurping it down like it was the last supper. I was moaning and all just to give him the full thrill. His ass was breathing hard and rubbing all over himself. To leave him wondering, I simply told him next time might be his lucky day. He smiled and slid the two Benjamin's in my back pocket as I got out of the car. Girl, I can't make this shit up."

Both Mia and Sky burst out laughing. Mia envisioned the whole scenario as she was watching a drama movie. Sky was wild like that. Mia wasn't far behind her with her level of shenanigans. They were so connected 'til the point that they fully trusted each other and if any of their dirt came out, they would be ready to defend and ride for each other. Their friendship consisted of loyalty and trust; and in the world of being the only child, that's just what Mia needed-- a sister.

Mia and Sky were so excited about Summer Jam. They spent hours getting their nails and hair done. They made sure their stuff was tight. In their naive minds, this was an investment. Mia hoped that Rossi would see her looking good at the Summer Jam, wife her, and she'd live her life as a rapper's lady. Sky, on the other hand, just wanted to be in the mix.

The girls were going all out for this concert. They had gotten their make-up done by a boy named

Kyle. Kyle lived one complex over from Sky and he did all the locals' make-up. If anybody wanted their face beat, they knew to hit up Kyle. Kyle, who was saving up for hormone pills and butt injections, used his talents to provide a steady income for himself. Only seventeen, he created a name for himself by doing make-up at the local strip clubs and in his mother's kitchen. His game was so on point that people ignored how messy he was, and others just wanted to be around him to get the latest news.

Mia had convinced Sky to ask Kyle to get his sister to let them buy their clothes from her. Instead of spending regular prices, they could save almost half of their money. Kyle's sister, Karmen, was a local booster. She took pride in stealing the latest trends and selling it for half the price.

Sky was down. Money saved was always the move.

Once Kyle finished their makeup, they went across the hall to Karmen's room. Mia was shocked at the range of clothing Karmen had in her room - Gucci, Prada, Dolce & Gabbana, Baby Phat, True Religion. Karmen had whatever you wanted. She had completely turned her bedroom to a functioning boutique. When she closed down shop for the day, she would pull her air mattress out of the hall closet and retire for the night.

Mia and Sky looked around the room with their eyes wide and mouths slightly hanging open as they scanned the room. There was no doubt about it. They were in designer heaven.

"Dang, Karmen! You are the plug!" Mia said.

"You know how I do," she exclaimed. Karmen was the flashy type. She wore a pink Nicki Minaj looking wig, fitted short skirt, colorful halter top, and gold hoop earrings with the matching wrist bangles. Like her brother, being flamboyant was their signature.

"See, I told you Sky. This was the move," Mia said.

"Ya'll bishes got lucky cuz the girls almost cleaned me out for this Summer Jam. I just re'd-up this morning. What you see is all new shit."

Mia browsed through some of the racks of clothes. Some of the stuff she had seen her classmates and their parents wear. She was blown away by the original tags. She picked up a pair of brown Jessica Simpson wedges with a price tag of $109.

"How much for these?" she asked.

Karmen squinted at the shoes and replied, "Those are the last pair and that's your size. Give me $35."

"Bet! Add this to my tab."

Mia continued searching. She needed to find the right attire for the concert, something that would catch Rossi's attention at first glance. She knew no basic outfit would do. A man like him required sophistication and sass. She wanted to look fly and be noticed by the future love of her life. Sadly, she was spending her baby daddy's drug money on an outfit for her new rapper boo.

"Can you believe we're about to be the hottest chicks at the concert tonight?" Sky asked as she observed a Juicy Couture purse.

"I can't freaking wait. The look on my future husband's face is going to be priceless when he sees me in the crowd."

"Yea, whatever," Sky retorted.

"Umm-hmm, you should send a pic to Dub and let him see how fly you look once we're all dressed."

"You're right huh? I should."

"Yup! My bestie gonna be breaking necks tonight. And, I see how you be blushing when that nigga sends you messages. You ain't gotta front with me. I know you feeling him," Mia said jokingly.

"I ain't saying all that but I guess I got a sweet spot for him. He does come through when I need him."

"Chick, he's doing more than coming through, he's dropping bank and wood."

Mia and Sky slapped hands and burst out into laughter. Sky was not revealing her hand about Dub but Mia knew her best friend and knew Dub was getting closer to Sky's soft spot. However, she knew Sky would never admit it. To Sky, boyfriends were overrated and just an extra emotional rollercoaster she wasn't down to ride.

They spent over an hour in Karmen's room trying to decide on the right look. Some things they wanted, Karmen didn't have their size or they couldn't afford it. Karmen was okay with them staying that long because she still had other girls coming and going. Nothing made Karmen feel better than to see the fruits of her labor generate income. At the end of most nights, Karmen cashed in at about $3,000 to $3,500.

Mia and Sky both locked in on their attire for the night. They spent a total of $275 which was well worth the coin. The things they got would cost well over $700 in the stores. They couldn't wait to slay tonight. They were like two kids who believed in Santa Clause. They were so excited they couldn't stop laughing and joking.

If they played their cards right, this was the come up to set them apart from all the other girls who were just playing the game.

It was the moment they both had been anticipating. They were in Sky's room that she shared with her younger sister. Sky's sisters were in the living room watching Players Club for the umpteenth time, her mother was probably at the casino, so they had the room to themselves. Mia was excited about the concert. All she could think about was how all eyes were going to be on her as she made her grand entrance. She had spoken to Drew earlier and all was well with them. She felt herself slowly pulling away from him but the further she pulled the harder he chased. It wasn't like Drew to give up money, so she knew things were getting serious on his end. All it took was one phone call and he was meeting her to give her money.

Sky had her desktop computer playing all the jams they were about to go sing along to at the concert. Sky was in the mirror with her bra and panties on while the speakers were playing their favorite jam by T.I. As they sang in unison to "Motivation", they both had separate thoughts.

Mia was glowing thinking about Rossi and Sky was thinking about mixing and mingling with the local ballers. Sky's only concern was to come up. It had nothing to do with cliché dream of chasing some rapper. Her only goal was to find someone ready to sponsor her.

POINT! BLANK! PERIOD!

Mia decided to wear an all-black fitted bodycon dress by Vera Wang. The details in the dress were crazy! The right arm had a full sleeve and the left arm was sleeveless. The dress was knee length; however, the left side had a high split that revealed the entire left thigh. She wore her Jessica Simpson wedges to provide feet support while standing the entire time.

Mia's silhouette was banging. Her innocent yet mature look was sure to pull off her mission. She kept her jewelry simple and wore a cross necklace and a small rope bracelet. Her hair was in a body wrap. She had it highlighted bronze to emphasize her mahogany skin. Mia's long voluptuous hair fell perfectly down her back, making her look foreign. She loved her hair. It gave her an older mature vibe.

Sky was a hairstylist at heart and always came through with her hair looks. She always changed her hairstyles to match her attire. And tonight was no different. She wanted to go all out! She didn't want to play it safe. So she wore a black fitted mini skirt with a Gucci belt around her small waist that exposed her thick thighs and plump ass. She wore a Gucci silk print blouse and left it half button to reveal her perky breaks and opted out of wearing a bra. Her oldest sister's Gucci single strap six-inch heels were planted on her feet to complete her attire. She decided to take out her braids and rocked two long butt length scalp braids to the back. She made sure her edges were laid!

Once both girls were finished, they walked into the living room looking like divas. With Karmen coming through with the threads and Kyle slaying their make-up, they were ready to display themselves like models.

"Look at ya'll young whores... Lookin' like ya'll going to a club instead of a concert," Sky's oldest sister, Serena said.

"Damn, Sky, you lookin' like you thirty," another one of Sky's sisters, Samantha added.

"I know them aren't my damn Gucci shoes! Did you ask could you borrow them?" Sky's second eldest sister, Stormie, questioned.

Sky rolled her eyes as if she was annoyed. She was ready to get out of the house. Her sisters were starting to get on her nerves.

"Serena, are you taking us to the concert?" Sky asked.

"Do ya'll have my gas money? Like I said earlier, you either going to pay me, a cab or get to hitchhiking."

"And you damn sure not hitchhiking in my damn Gucci shoes," Sky's sister Stormie chimed in.

Sky sucked her teeth, "Yeah, we got your money now let's go."

After waiting another ten minutes for Serena to finish watching Ebony get beat up by Diamond, the girls were finally ready to go.

Chapter 7

*T*hey finally made it to the coliseum. With all the traffic, it took them over forty-five minutes to make it to the entrance. Cars were at a standstill, people were trying to find or make their parks, and some weren't even trying to attend the concert, they just got out to be seen and see who else was out. Luckily for them, they were getting dropped off, so it eliminated the headache of parking.

It was a humid Sunday night and they were grateful the people scanning tickets were moving with precision. Unlike Sky, who had braids, Mia didn't want her hair to frizz before getting the chance to sweat it out. Mia noticed the tour buses, the expensive cars, and trailers that were parked at the back entrance. So many people came out to attend the Summer Jam.

Mia and Sky weren't the only ones who came dressed to kill. There were all types of women - old and young. They were dressed just as provocative, if not more. They had the same thoughts: get chosen or prove why they should be chosen.

The fellas didn't come short stopping either. They knew what time it was, too. Men came dressed in their D-boy clothes and jewelry. The more they flossed, the more women thought they had it. But Sky could see right through their cheap cologne and borrowed outfits.

They finally made it past security and into the coliseum. Like usual, Sky wanted to do a once over of her outfit, so she dragged Mia to the restroom. Mia knew her stuff was tight, so she waited for Sky at the restroom's entrance. Someone bumped into her while they were exiting.

"Oh, I'm so sorry. Excuse me for not paying attention."

"Justice!" Mia yelled.

"Mia! Oh my God! Girl, how are you doing?" Justice asked.

"Who would have thought we'd see each other so soon."

"I know right. You lookin' good girl. Just last week we were handling business now we are out partying. Ain't it funny how things turn out," Justice confessed.

"Who are you here with? I know you are not alone. Are you?"

"No. I'm here with my best friend. Who are you here with?"

"Girl I came with an entourage. Most of the girls I work with at the club are here. The promoter of the concert invited us to show the rappers a good time."

"What!" Mia squealed.

Mia finally noticed the VIP tag around Justice's neck. A light bulb quickly went off in Mia's head. Mia was now trying to find out how she and Sky could be a part of the VIP squad. Mia looked at Justice for the first time. Her current look was the total opposite of the hospital gown she met her in. Justice had on a red mesh see-through jumper with clear 8-inch stilettos. She had on a blonde wig with fire red lipstick. Her whole ensemble screamed stripper.

Sky came out of the restroom to see Mia talking to someone. She had never seen this person before. Sky wasn't the jealous type, but she saw all kinds of red flags with this mystery person.

"Justice, this is my best friend I was telling you about, Sky," Mia said in excitement.

"Nice to meet you. Girl you wearing the hell out of that outfit. Baby, you got taste," Justice proclaimed.

"Well thank you. It's nice to meet you, too. Even though I haven't heard anything about you," Sky said with sarcasm.

"Sky, Justice was just telling me how she is VIP and is entertaining the rappers until they perform," Mia loosely said.

Sky picking up on what Mia was putting down quickly picked up her mood and intentionally tried to form an ally with Justice.

"Oh really? Think you all have room for two more?" Sky asked with a smile.

"I'm sure I can work my magic." Justice winked. "Pete always believes the more the merrier."

"Who's Pete?" Mia asked.

"He's the club promoter who hired us."

Mia and Sky looked at each other like, *what the hell are we getting ourselves into*. Never the ones to reject an offer, they were ready to get themselves backstage. If anything was to pop-off, they would move accordingly. But now, their only motive was to get backstage.

They followed Justice to the back of the stage. They walked down a long foyer before they made it to her room. There were so many people that almost every step they were saying, "Excuse me." Security guards were on high alert with their walkies on their hips and headphones in their ears. Nothing appeared to be getting past them. The host, Jay Man, was on stage warming up the crowd. You could hear the crowd laughing and the DJ teasing them by playing snippets of the artist's songs.

Once they made it to the door, Justice turned to them and said, "Look, in here I go by Tender. I know ya'll young and shit and trying to act older but here is where the real acting begins. So get all that young girl shit out your heads. If they ask you how old you are, say you are seventeen. This is not the movie, this the real deal. Niggas in here will try you and because I feel like I am bringing you in, I feel a level of protection over you. Check yourselves now and make sure you are ready for what's on the other side of the door. Are we clear?"

Justice laid it on thick. She wanted to make sure they were ready for what they've been asking for. That young and innocent mentality was out the door. It was time to step up or go take their seats with the other patrons.

Mia and Sky both looked at each other and said the only thing they knew to say, "Yes."

Justice didn't say anything else to them. She simply turned around and opened the door. The room was so foggy due to the weed smoke. Mia and Sky were nervous but a fly on the wall couldn't tell. They walked behind Justice with confidence. They acted unfazed to the girls half naked and hearing the rappers call the girls bitches and hoes.

While in stride, Mia looked around to see if she saw Rossi. She was yearning to see his full lips and sexy smile. She just knew he was somewhere to be found. Unfortunately, the further they got into the room there was no sign of Rossi.

Mia and Sky noticed a few of the local rappers. There were no mainstream rappers in the room. Sky stopped Justice and asked what Mia was thinking, "Where is Young Jeezy and 'nem?"

"They're in the room over there." Justice pointed towards a room with a closed door. "You have to get chosen to go in there. What happens is, their bodyguard or a member of their team will come over, scout girls, and ask you to follow them. That's the way it goes," Justice said in a whisper.

Mia took an inconspicuous look around the room. The room reeked of sex, weed, and a faint stitch of an unfamiliar odor. Two girls were making out on the couch. The girls were engaged in an intense kiss and fondling each other's breasts while sitting side by side. If Mia had to guess, they were putting on a show to be one of the few to be chosen to go to the next room.

This was beyond Mia's wildest dream. There was no way she would have guessed this took place or even guessed that she would be backstage witnessing this. Mia looked over at Sky who appeared comfortable. She leaned on the wall with her legs crossed at the ankles and her arms folded. Sky blended but she had this no-nonsense look on her face. Mia decided to sit on one of the black leather couches. One of the girls next to her was snorting what appeared to be cocaine off the end table. She had a dollar bill tightly rolled seemingly between her thumb and index finger. She bent down and took another sniff. She must've sniffed too hard because she leaned back and pinched the brim of her nose. She looked over at Mia who was staring intensely at her. The girl looked to be Mia's age but under all her makeup, Mia had a hard time gauging her age.

"You want some?" The girl sluggishly asked.

"Nah."

"Then what the fuck you staring at?"

Mia turned away and tried to focus her eyes on the floor.

"I want you, you, and you. Come with me," one of the bodyguards stated as he pointed at Mia, Sky, and another girl. The girl rushed past Mia so fast that she bumped into her shoulder. Justice walked over to Mia and Sky looking like a proud mother who was watching her girls go off to prom.

"Remember what I told you. If you not ready for what's on the other side of the door, now is the time to run because don't nobody want to hear no. Suck it up or leave now."

Justice laid it all on the line. She read Mia and Sky's thoughts and knew exactly what their next move was.

"Look, take my number. Text me if you need me." Justice slipped her number in Mia's clutch.

Mia felt that Justice cared for her. It was like an older sister she never had, and she respected Justice for that.

Mia and Sky followed the bodyguard to the other room. The show had begun and some of the opening acts have started performing. Each room had the show projected on large TVs. It let the next act know when it was close to their time to go on. When they walked into the next room, Mia and Sky were both instantly star struck. In the center of the room sat T.I. who was in deep conversation with Lil Boosie and Young Jeezy. They were so unfazed by their entrance that no one even stopped to take notice. The bodyguard instructed them to have a seat. Before they entered the room, the bodyguard had already given them the dos and don'ts. The girls had to agree before they even entered the room.

Mia's heart was pounding outside of her chest. She just knew that someone heard it. To intensify her racing heart, Rossi strolled out of the restroom. There stood Rossi with his perfect smile and hearty laugh. She just couldn't believe her luck. Sky must've felt her energy and nudged to say, "Bitch get your shit together."

Rossi looked over at the girls engaging in small talk. He and Mia shared eye contact for a split second. He recognized her from several encounters. His first thought was, *What the hell is she doing here?*

Mia felt the knot in her stomach. Aside from being ten feet from her favorite artist, T.I., she was also ten feet away from her soulmate. It was becoming harder for her to suppress her excitement. To help take off the edge, Mia got up and poured herself a shot of Vodka. She felt so anxious that she found herself taking three.

"Whhooa... whhooaa. Slow down there. What's got you killing the bottle like that?"

Rossi stood behind Mia at the bar. She couldn't believe he was so close to her. The hairs on the back of her neck stood at attention. His Bond No.9 cologne drowned her nostrils. The smell sent tingles down her spine that led to moisture in her panties. Mia had to gather her thoughts because this was her moment. This was what she fantasized about.

Mia slowly turned around and she was nose to nose with Rossi. The cologne drowning her nose drove her insane.

"I just needed something to take the edge off. It might be a long night. Just never know."

"Like that?"

"Yeah!"

"Don't nothing come fast but a crash. Pace yourself."

Rossi's words were like gold to Mia. He could have told her to keep drinking and she would have. It just felt so surreal to her. His words were so mature, and nothing compared to how Drew talked to her. She wanted more and she wasn't going to let him walk away without exchanging numbers or some type of connection.

Mia noticed Sky mingling with Lil' Boosie. Whatever he was saying had her dying laughing because the room was filled with her laughter and his jokes.

"Rossi, you're up in ten," one of the bodyguards yelled.

"Yo, you're going to be here when I get back?" Rossi asked.

"Only if you want me to be."

"Fa sho." Those words were like bondage to Mia.

Mia watched Rossi on stage from the TV monitor backstage. Of course, she knew all his songs and couldn't believe her luck. She went from thinking she was going to be front and centered on the front row to watch it all unfold from right in the backstage suite. Rossi looked so good with his black and white Givenchy tracksuit and all-white Givenchy sneakers. He rocked the crowd as if he was the headliner.

Being a local, the entire crowd knew Rossi's music. He finished his set with his latest classic "Come Thru". Everyone screamed. The song was a ladies' anthem. The savvy and smooth vibe of the lyrics had the ladies grinding and gyrating. Mia pictured herself being the one he was asking to come through. She too moved her hips to the beat backstage. Rossi definitely gave the crowd their money's worth.

Rossi and his crew returned backstage and he was like a legend within his rights. Other artists dapped him up and saluted him on a job well done. Rossi was so chill and reserved that he didn't show much emotions. He shook a few hands and gave a couple of head nods.

Mia acted like she was engaged in conversation with a few other girls who were backstage while Sky entertained a few of the artists. Mia didn't want to seem too occupied and she didn't want Rossi to see her talking to other guys. She wanted him to see she was available. Mia saw Rossi's crew gathering his things as if they were preparing to leave. Her heart was beating so loud it could have been heard out of her chest. She could barely focus on what the girls were saying. She was too busy watching Rossi.

As she turned around, she saw Rossi leave with a few members of his crew. She instantly felt saddened. She needed to take a seat. This was not what she hoped for. Mia walked back to her seat, sat down, crossed her legs, and scanned the room. A few moments later, some tall, dark-skinned guy stood over Mia and tapped her shoulder.

"Aye, Rossi wants you to meet him in his car. Grab your stuff. You're rolling with us," one of Rossi's guards told Mia.

Mia barely could contain her smile. This was by far better than anything she could ever imagine. Mia looked around to find Sky. She gave Sky their code gesture, which was a swipe over the brow. Sky returned the gesture. They came up with this move to let the other know – game time.

Mia walked outside of the coliseum and there was a hint of a cool breeze in the air. The parking lot was still thick, as the concert continued to play out. She looked in the sky and took a deep sigh. The air was just what she needed. Backstage, the walls felt like they were caving in. She was grateful for the fresh air.

The guard opened the back door to the all-white Yukon Denali and Mia slid in. To her surprise, Rossi wasn't inside. It was only her and the driver. Mia looked confused. Before she could speak, the guard said, "He'll be out soon," and abruptly shut the door.

Mia looked around the truck and tried to peep out the window, but the windows were so tinted everything looked darker than it was. She tried to relax but it was hard to do knowing that she was about to have her first alone time with the man of her dreams.

Forty-five minutes later Rossi was let into the truck with a briefcase in one hand and his phone in the other. He leaned up and whispered something to the driver and the driver quickly nodded. He looked at Mia and smiled and she nervously smiled back. He turned around and put the briefcase on the floor of the third row of the Denali. Mia assumed it was filled with money he had made from the night. His cologne, once again, sent Mia into paralysis. Controlling her emotions was extremely hard to do this close to Rossi. She was never like this around Drew. She was always confident and in control. But Rossi was on a different level. His status alone was intimidating.

"You hungry? It's pretty late but I know a spot that would hook us up a plate or two," Rossi said as he looked at his Movado watch.

The words wouldn't come out and all she could do was nod. Rossi chuckled.

"Take us to the spot," Rossi ordered while looking at Mia.

"What's so funny?" Mia asked as she looked slightly at Rossi.

"You! You all over there tense and shit. Don't act like you shy," he stated while laughing.

"Trust me I'm not. You must think you a celebrity or somethin'?"

"Nah I am just a regular guy," Rossi said while maintaining his smile.

"Good. Cause I'm just a regular girl who likes regular guys."

"Is that right. So tell me something good."

"What you want to know?" Mia asked as she turned to face Rossi. She was gaining confidence with each statement she let out.

"Like, what's your story? Who's at home waiting for you?" Rossi added while rubbing the hairs on his chin.

"I'm with you. There's no reason to ask about home. I should be asking you the same thing, Mr. Rossi."

"I like that. I'm stealing that. I'm with you and that's enough for both of us now. Let's keep that vibe for the night."

Mia looked at him square in his eyes and said, "Bet."

Mia and Rossi made it to the place he called, The Spot. They entered through the side of the place which was directly through the kitchen. He led the way with the briefcase in his left hand and Mia's hand in his right. Once inside, Rossi passed someone the briefcase and they retreated with the briefcase in hand.

"So what you want to eat, sexy? Whatever you craving, my cook can make it for you."

"Your cook? Is this your spot Mr. Rossi?" Mia asked with a slight grin.

Rossi smirked. Before responding, Rossi turned and ordered the bartender to make two drinks. He walked over with his cool stride and turned on some music. The speakers blared Bootsy Collins song "I'd Rather Be With You". The baritone of Boosty's voice staged the scene.

"You guessed it. I opened this bar a few years ago. I call it Blue. It's like Switzerland in the streets. Anybody can come here and know it's safe and they're good. Before all this rap stuff took off, I was doing other things to make sure my family ate and once I had enough, I wanted to make sure everybody ate," Rossi said as he took a sip of his Cognac.

"Wow, I had no clue. That's admirable."

There was a long pause. It was if they both were in deep thought vibing to the tunes of Bootsy. Rossi continued to sip his drink and Mia just maintained her gaze to not make contact.

Mia put her hand on Rossi's shoulder and looked at him and said, "I am proud of you." Without saying a word, Rossi leaned in and kissed Mia. It wasn't a French kiss and it wasn't a deep kiss. It was passionate and simple, but it spoke volumes.

"I know you're too young for me, yo. But you make sure you keep shit real and once the time is right, we'll be what is meant to be."

Rossi's statement took Mia aback. She wasn't expecting Rossi to say that. She didn't even know if he knew her age or not. She was now embarrassed. She had no clue what he thought of her and felt like he could see right through her which was a scary thing.

His words kept echoing in her mind. She tried to relax the rest of the night, but her words became less confident.

Dang, so long for a relationship with him, Mia thought.

Chapter 8

M ia woke up at the foot of Sky's bed while Sky was at the head of the bed. When they woke up it was 2 pm the next day. They couldn't believe they had slept that long. Heck, neither of them could believe their night. Rossi dropped Mia off at Sky's about 4 am and Sky made it in shortly after her. Sky had spent the rest of the night with a few of the girls from the concert and Lil' Boosie's entourage. After the concert, they rode on the bus to the afterparty at Upper-Level nightclub where Lil' Boosie did an appearance.

"Girl I had the night of my life! I wish you were there. Hell, I wish I could've had pictures to remember the night. Too bad we couldn't have our phones, huh? Shit was live at the after spot. I saw so many people we knew, and they saw me shining in VIP with Lil' Boosie looking like a bag of money. It was off the chain!" Sky said in excitement as she bounced up and down in the bed.

"Umph. Good for you!"

"Bitch why you being a sour puss? What's the tea with you and Rossi? Give me all the details."

"Ain't nothing to tell."

"You can stop holding out cause I know it went down. Let me hear."

"I said, it ain't nothing to tell," Mia said as she sucked her teeth.

"Damn, what's wrong with you? This was supposed to be the night of your life."

"Well, it wasn't. We left and went to his bar, talked, he kissed me, we ate, and he brought me here. That's it!"

"Wait! Rossi got a damn bar? Ya'll kissed? This doesn't sound like nothing to me."

"He had the nerve to tell me one day I can be his girl, but he knows I am too young for him. If he knew all that shit, then why he even ask me to leave with him? I feel so stupid, Sky."

"Dang girl. That's cold," Sky said shaking her head.

"It must be something there because ain't no way he still invited you to his spot and not feel nothing for you."

"That's how niggas are. They play too many games, Sky. That's why I'm still doing me, ya know."

"Ok well check this out, some folks from Lil' Boosie's entourage invited us down to Louisiana to a pool party. We should get us a rental and slide down there for the weekend."

"Oh shit, I might've missed the hype last night, but I am not missing out this time around. How are we gonna get a car?"

"So I was thinking, you still be talking to the store owner, Tony?"

"Yeah, now and then. Why?"

"Good. So since he has a soft spot for you, I was thinking that you call him up and get him to rent us a car."

"You must've bumped your head. That man isn't going to get us a car and you crazy if you think I'm gonna have sex with him just to get a car," Mia said while shaking her head.

"Look, all you got to do is charm and sweet talk him. Make him *think* you are gonna have sex with him once you get back. You know he likes you and he is always giving you money out of the blue. You just have to be extra persuasive this time," Sky said as she poured it on thick to Mia.

Mia thought about it. This could work.

Tony was a convenience store owner in Sky's neighborhood. He was a fat bald head guy who had a sweet tooth for younger girls. Despite being married, he felt more like himself when he was wooing and coercing some young girl to be his secret. Mia had been talking to Tony for a while. They started talking a little after she met Drew. It initially started with a little flirting and after hearing the rumors of how fruitful he was with his money, Mia made it her business to milk the cow as long as she could. She would get one to three hundred dollars at a time. They would text or she would visit him at the store, but it never went past that. What Sky was asking Mia to do was risky. This was bigger than a couple of hundred dollars. She didn't know how Tony was going to respond but if they wanted to go to Louisiana in style, she had to step her wordplay up. This was a task she was up for.

"Okay. See if you can get your mom's car. We going to the store," Mia stated in confidence.

Sky looked at Mia in approval.

———————————•◦•———————————

Mia had texted Tony and let him know that she was coming to see him. Like always, he was waiting for her arrival. Mia walked into the old convenience store and immediately locked eyes with Tony behind the cash register. They were separated by a thick bulletproof glass. Mia nodded towards the back which suggested that she wanted him to meet her in his office.

Mia waited for him in his chair. Tony walked into the office with a white dingy shirt and blue jean shorts. He had on cheap no-slip black tennis shoes and smelled like Cool Water cologne. Mia almost gagged when he hugged her. She couldn't believe what she was about to ask him. Heck, she couldn't believe that she was talking to him at all.

"Hey, beautiful. How are you? I'm surprised to see you today. You must was thinking about me," Tony said.

"You shouldn't be surprised. You know I try to see you every chance I get."

Tony smiled and guided her up so she could sit in his lap.

"Is that so?"

"Yup," Mia replied with a forced smile.

"So what's up. Tell me something good."

"Well, it's been a slow summer for me. My mom has been sick, so I have been in the house a lot lately making sure she's good while my dad works."

"I'm sorry to hear that. I'm even more sorry that you aren't having a good summer. Someone as beautiful as you should be enjoying herself. Maybe at the pool with a sexy swimsuit on," Tony said as he ran his hands from the top to the bottom of her back. Mia cringed at his touch. She didn't try to, but her reflex took over.

"You're right. That's why I came to see you. I need a favor."

"Anything beautiful. What can I do for you?"

"I need you to rent me a car. I want to go to Louisiana to Blue Bayou. I just need to go clear my head and try to have some fun."

"That's a big request that you are asking of me."

Mia put her head down and began to talk in a low tone. "I know. I had no one else to ask. Since we've been talking, I made it my business to not talk to anyone else."

Tony now had his hand on Mia's butt and the other on her thigh. Mia knew she had to talk fast before he got any ideas.

"So, you want me to do this huuugggge favor for you, but you have never done anything for me. Why should I?"

"I thought our relationship wasn't based on that. I thought we had something different. I mean I am willing to go there with you, but I need to see if you trust me as much as I trust you. What if I give it to you and you stop being there for me. I'll be devastated," Mia suggested.

Tony continued to rub Mia's ass and he was quiet for a while. Mia was about to get up and leave because she refused to beg him. It wasn't that serious to her and she knew she wasn't going to have sex with him for the car. It would take more than a car to get her to have sex with him. We were talking thousands! If Sky wanted to go to Louisiana that bad, she was going to have to come up with another trick.

"A'ight. I'm willing to get the car for you but under one condition."

Mia couldn't contain her excitement on the inside. She was ready to say yes to whatever proposition he was about to propose.

"I'm listening," she said coolly.

"When you get back you have to show Tony just how much you value him. No excuses."

Mia hurriedly said, "Done!"

Mia began to turn the knob to walk out of his office, but Tony stopped it with his heavy foot.

He looked down at her and said, "next time you lie to me like you aren't talking to no one else, I won't be so nice. Streets talk and I know about your little fling with that boy, Drew. That's not a concern to me but don't give me a lie I didn't ask for."

Tony moved his foot and Mia dang near ran out of his office and store.

Once inside of Sky's mom's car, Mia held her head down.

"What girl? Talk to me. What did he say?!" Sky yelled.

Mia sat still and shook her head. Sky sat back in her seat and hit the steering wheel.

"That fat pervert," Sky said.

"BITTCCHH, WE ARE GOING TO LOUISIANA!" Mia screamed in excitement.

———●———

It was time to meet Tony to get the rental car. He instructed her that the car would be at one of the gas pumps and the key would be in the armrest. Of course, she had to play nice and talk all lovey-dovey with him. She was able to get some gas and spending money from him which was a little over $350. He said it was all he had in cash; so he gave her everything in his pocket. Mia was happy with that and dared not to complain. Mia told her parents that she was going to

Louisiana with Sky and her older sister to Blue Bayou. Like usual, they didn't bother to call Sky's mother to verify. Mia never understood how they trusted her so much even after all she had done. However, it wasn't her job to play the child and the parent. That was on them. Her father had given her $200 and Grandma Rose had given her another $200 for spending money. Mia had a total of $750. This was more than enough for a cheap motel, gas, and food. Sky was also able to rack in with Dub. As much as she downplayed their relationship, Mia knew Sky liked Dub.

Mia had been thinking about her encounter with Rossi. They didn't exchange numbers and she wished she could pull up on him so he could see her on her grown woman shit. She and Drew were still talking but he was doing more talking to her than she was to him. She didn't want a relationship with him. If she couldn't be with Rossi, she wanted to do just what she and Sky were doing - playing the game.

Tony had done well. He got them a 2005 Silver Chevy Cobalt. It looked just like them. He had added Mia as a driver. He told Hertz rental that she was his daughter who was going out of town for the weekend. She didn't care if he told them she was his wife, she just wanted the car.

Sky had Dub drop them off at the store. They got into the car and immediately popped in a mix cd that had all their favorite jams on it. They felt like divas. With their shades on, Mia pulled off headed I-10 by 10. Sky had been texting one of the guys from Lil' Boosie's crew. He had given Sky the address to the pool party and gotten them a hotel at the Marriott not too far from where the pool party would be.

Once they made it, they went immediately to the hotel to change into their swimsuits that they had gotten from Karmen. Mia had spent $100 on a two-piece Fendi swimsuit and Sky ended up finding a Gucci one-piece swimsuit. Since shopping at Karmen's, all they have been wearing was designer. It was like they were slowly coming into their own and learning the hustle quickly.

Mia and Sky made it to the pool party looking stunning. They blended well with the older women who were there. They didn't look like two fourteen-year-old girls who were on the wrong side of the streets. They talked the talk and walked the walk. They could hang with the best of them. From style to conversation, to street-savvy, they belonged and made sure everyone knew it. The sun radiated on their melanated skin, adding fuel to their confidence.

"Hey, Sky. Is this your friend, Mia?"

"Yes, Hey Kross. Mia, this is Kross. Kross is the one who invited us here."

"Nice to meet you," Mia said as she reached to shake Kross' hand.

Mia noticed how fine Kross was. He appeared to be in his late 20s' but age never meant anything to them. His chiseled abs and red Tommy Hilfiger shorts made him look exotic. Mia needed to know the scoop about him and Sky before she got too flirty.

"Where's my manners. Would you ladies like something to drink?"

"Sure," Sky said.

Not trusting anyone to make their drinks, they both followed Kross to the bartender inside the patio. Mia looked around. It was a private party. It was about ten girls which included them and about fifteen guys. It could've been more, but Mia only counted that many. No one was allowed into the house. The furthest you could go was the pool and to the restroom that was connected to the patio. Mia hadn't spotted Lil' Boosie and was questioning if this really a Lil' Boosie's party. Mia made eye contact with Sky and they both thought the same thing.

"So, who's party is this?" Sky asked Kross.
Kross took a sip from his drink and said, "It's the big homie's."

Mia and Sky looked at each other and then looked back at Kross. "Who the hell is big homie?" they asked in unison.

"Oh, my bad. Lil' Boosie's," Kross said in laughter.

Mia and Sky laughed, too.

"Where is he?" Mia asked.

"He's coming. Knowing him, he's probably trying to make an entrance. He's right upstairs. This is his house here in Baton Rouge."

Mia and Sky began drinking and enjoying the company of Kross. The sun was now setting, and they were having the time of their life. By now, Lil' Boosie had joined the party and everyone treated him like he was regular. No one overcrowded him or acted like groupies, which Mia liked. She hated to see people act starstruck around celebrities. It was weird to her.

"How did ya'll like ya'll hotel?" Kross asked.

"It's nice. Thank you again for that," Sky added.

"No problem. I couldn't have two sexy ladies come down and not show them a good time. I hope you all are having a good time," Kross quizzed.

"Yes, I love the vibe," Mia said.

"Great. I think you both are beautiful," Kross said as he began to slur his words. His hands were now gliding down both their backs. Mia and Sky both side-stepped to release his touch.

"I think you all should kiss."

"Excuse me?" Sky retorted.

"I said I think ya'll should kiss."

"Nah, you gotta be tripping," Mia replied.

"Nah, I think you tripping. The first time I asked, this time I am telling you," Kross said with a sinister tone.

Mia was becoming uncomfortable. She walked away with Sky right on her heels.

Kross didn't take too well to rejection so he followed behind them and pulled both of them by their arms.

"What the fuck is wrong with ya'll? You think you gonna walk away from me like I am some fucking peon?"

Both of them winced in pain. "Kross you are hurting us. Let us go!" Mia yelled.

"Oh so now you can hear me. You bitches kill me. Try to show you hoes a good time, but I see ya'll don't know your place."

Kross had a tight grip on both of their arms. Mia was now scared. Clearly, others could see what was going on, but no one stepped in to deescalate the situation. Mia began to panic. She didn't know what to do and they were too far from home for some shit to go down.

"Okay! Okay! Follow us in our car. I am too shy to kiss her in public," Sky said confidently.

Mia thought Sky was stupid. It was dark in the front of the house and she knew no one was up there to witness anything if something went down.

"That's more like it. I'm gon' hold ya'll in case ya'll try something stupid."

They walked to the front of the house to their parked car. Still not knowing what Sky had up her sleeve, Mia was scared and felt like she wasn't in control. She kept trying to look out the corner of her eye for a sign from Sky, but she just kept looking straight.

"Okay, go ahead," Kross said letting them know they should kiss. He took a step back to observe them.

He appeared relaxed and the sweat on the tip of his brow gave him a grueling look.

Sky leaned in to kiss Mia. Mia took a step back thinking Sky was crazy. Sky winked at Mia. Whatever Sky had planned that was her way of telling Mia to fall in line. Again, Sky leaned in to kiss Mia. With her back facing the car and her hands behind her back, Sky began to open her purse, discreetly.

"Yeah, that's it. Go 'head and do what daddy sa...."

PSSST!!

Before Kross could finish, Sky was spraying mace in his eyes.

"RUN!" Sky yelled at Mia.

"*AGGHHHH!*" Kross yelped. "You dumb ungrateful bitches!"

Mia ran to the other side of the car and was so thankful Sky had already had the key in the ignition. Mia hurriedly turned the car and jerked the car in drive. While taking off, they heard Kross scream, "You dumb bitches! I'm going to kill both of you."

Petal to the metal Mia was driving like a madwoman. Not knowing where they were going, she was scared and driving recklessly.

"Pull over up there and stop at that store," Sky said as she pointed to a gas station ahead.

"Are you crazy? I am not pulling over," Mia said in a panic.

"Look, you got to pull over at the store. We have to put the hotel on the GPS so we can get our things."

Mia pulled over at the Chevron and opened the door. As soon as she got out, she immediately threw up. The smell of mace and the feeling of fear was too much for her. Sky walked around the car to help Mia.

"Look, we're good. Gather yourself because we have to get our things out of the hotel and go find our spot for the night. You get on the passenger side and I'll drive."

Sky took over the situation like a black girl who refused to die in a horror movie. Mia got into the passenger seat but appeared to be a nervous wreck.

"Just read the GPS to me," Sky told Mia. "You got to pull yourself together, Mia. That's the only way we are gonna get out of this."

Mia guided Sky to the Marriott hotel. Because it was so close to the pool party, they didn't have far to go. Sky parked the car in front of the hotel, and they dashed for the elevator. Both of them were running off pure adrenaline. They took the elevator to the 5th floor and ran to their hotel room.

Once inside, they grabbed their loose clothing items and stuffed them into their suitcase. Thankfully they were still packed from earlier and they only needed to grab clothes they had on previously. Not caring to change out of their swimsuits, they were out as quickly as they entered.

Mia felt the vibration of her phone. She looked down to see who was calling and the screen read:

Incoming: Rossi

Mia's heart stopped. *How did he get my number? More importantly, why is he calling me?* Mia thought.

In the midst of her thoughts, she noticed Sky had stopped running. She turned to see Sky looking like a deer in headlights. Mia forcefully turned around and gasped. It was the devil himself standing in front of them.

Kross was less than 30 feet in front of them with his fist clenched tight and his eye bloodshot red. Mia and Sky were completely speechless. Mia's phone continued to vibrate in her hand.

Incoming: Rossi

To be continued…....

Acknowledgements

Giving honor to God whom all blessings flow. Wow, I cannot believe my dream is now a reality. I remember writing on notebook paper in my Biology class, 11th grade, and letting my crew 'The Hot Girls' read my material. I have come a long way since then. It was time the world got a taste of what I have been itching to write.

To my daughter, Ivory Rose Glass, you are the rose that keeps mommy growing. I promise to show you and teach you how to be a beautiful melanated queen.

David Glass Jr., my wonderful and supportive husband, you are the push behind my dreams and the glue that helps make it all stick. The sacrifices you've made to make sure every goal I set out is accomplished, I can't thank you enough.

Shannon Walden, my beautiful mother, you are deserving of the world and one day I will make it my goal to bring you the biggest piece of it I can carry. Your tenacity is admirable.

To all of my friends and family, when I told you I was writing my first novel, I received nothing but positive words of encouragement. God has truly blessed me with an awesome circle. Your effortless support and love are what motivates me the most. May peace and love be with you all.

Lastly, to you my readers, stay tuned this is just the beginning. Lots of love... MUAH!

About the Author

———•———

Jessica Sherrell is a native of Jackson, MS but currently resides in Richmond, TX with her spouse and beautiful daughter. She holds a Bachelor of Science in Psychology from Mississippi State University and a Master of Arts in Clinical-Community Psychology from Texas Southern University. Jessica Sherrell spends her career advocating for mental health but enjoys the creativity writing urban fiction gives her.

Aside from her professional career, Jessica Sherrell enjoys spending time with friends and family, traveling, writing, attending church, and socializing. She always had a passion for writing, and it wasn't until her spouse pushed her to pursue dreams did, she really decide to show the world her talents.

If Only They Knew started from things she depicted in her childhood. Growing up in Jackson, MS, she was no stranger to the world around her. She wanted to depict what it was really like from her reality.

"No one writes about Mississippi. So much culture starts in the south and I wanted to do my part to fictionalize it"-
Jessica Sherrell

Connect with Jessica at www.authorjessicasherrell.com